AND THE
EXPLODING POPCORN MYSTERY

Discover more fun with Ollie Spark in . . .

AND THE
EXPLODING POPCORN MYSTERY

GILLIAN CROSS
AND ALAN SNOW

David Fickling Books

31 Beaumont Street
Oxford OX1 2NP, UK

Ollie Spark and the Exploding Popcorn Mystery
is a
DAVID FICKLING BOOK

First published in Great Britain in 2023 by
David Fickling Books,
31 Beaumont Street,
Oxford, OX1 2NP

www.davidficklingbooks.com

Text © Gillian Cross, 2023
Illustrations © Alan Snow, 2023

978-1-78845-241-0

1 3 5 7 9 10 8 6 4 2

Papers used by David Fickling Books are from well-
managed forests and other responsible sources.

DAVID FICKLING BOOKS Reg. No. 8340307

A CIP catalogue record for this book is available from the British Library.

Printed and bound in Great Britain by Clays, Ltd, Elcograf S.p.A.

To Mirabella
G.C.

To Annie-May, Betsy, Sophia and Errol
A.S.

Chapter 1
It's Aunt Caz!

'Ollie!' All my little cousins were yelling at once. 'Look at this!'

Gasket started barking and nudging my leg. He could hear how excited they were.

'Wait a minute!' I yelled back. The kitchen sink was blocked, and I was underneath it, unscrewing the trap.

'No, Ollie! You've got to come *now*! AUNT CAZ IS ON TV!'

'What?!' I dropped the trap and shoved a bowl under the open pipe. Then Gasket and I raced into the living room.

Everyone else in the family was squashed in there, staring at the TV screen. It was filled with . . . Aunt Caz! She was beaming and holding up a gigantic golden trophy.

'I never *dreamt* I'd win!' she was saying. 'I haven't even told my family I was shortlisted.'

'She's won Best Spy Book of the Year!' whispered Aunt Dionne.

The camera switched to the interviewer. He was beaming too. 'We all love Beddington Potts!' he said. 'Everyone wants to know – what's his next adventure?'

Aunt Caz's eyes gleamed. 'I've got a really great idea! He's going to travel to –'

. . . FJKE*!!!ORN^^*##WSNL%^ . . .

Oh no! The sound was going. The TV picture was breaking up.

'Ollie! Fix it!' everyone yelled.

But before I could move, the screen went black. For a second, the room was totally silent. Then my littlest cousin, Arabella, started to wail.

'It's not FAIR! I want to see Aunt Caz! Ollie, make the picture come back!'

I shook my head. 'Sorry. I think it's a power cut.'

All the cousins started wailing. For a second, the noise was so loud I thought my cardrums would burst. Then Uncle Marek stood up and clapped his hands.

'Get your trainers on! Quick!' he said. 'We'll go down to the park and play football.'

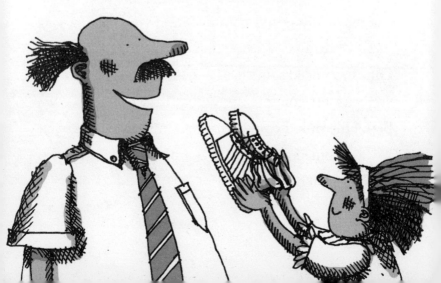

'YAY!' The cousins stopped wailing and scrambled off to find their trainers.

Uncle Marek waved his hand at me. 'You too, Ollie. You need some fun.'

I was just going to say 'Great!' – when I remembered the sink. I couldn't go out and leave it the way it was. Someone was sure to turn on the taps and flood the kitchen.

'I'll come later on,' I said. 'I just need to fix something first.'

I went back to the kitchen and unblocked the trap. As I fitted it back into place, I wasn't thinking about football. I was thinking about Beddington Potts. And the gleam in Aunt Caz's eyes.

'She's got another idea, Gasket,' I said. 'What d'you think it is?'

Would it cause as much trouble as the last one . . . ?

Chapter 2
The Really
Great Idea

We couldn't wait for Aunt Caz to come home! She kept sending messages, but it was three days before we heard her battered old van come lurching down the road. Its brakes squealed as she pulled up in front of the house.

'Look, everybody!' She jumped out of the van, waving the trophy above her head. 'Beddington Potts is Top Spy! I WON!'

Arabella raced out of the house and threw herself

at Aunt Caz, hugging her round the knees. 'We played football and I got THREE GOALS!'

Aunt Caz scooped her up with her free arm, chanting, 'We are the champions!'

We all went wild, clapping and cheering, with everyone talking at the same time.

'What was it like being on TV?'

'Could you see yourself?'

'We lost the picture cos of a power cut.'

'Did you win a million pounds?'

'You're brilliant!'

Aunt Caz stood there, grinning all over her face. She lifted her hands up, to make everyone listen. 'I didn't win a million pounds. But I did win some money. And this trophy. *And* . . . this!'

She put Arabella down and opened the side door of the van. Inside was the MOST ENORMOUS CAKE I'D EVER SEEN. It had three layers, was covered in green icing, and decorated with pink jelly fingerprints and chocolate false moustaches.

Aunt Caz waved her trophy again. 'Bring the cake

inside, Ollie – and we'll all have some!'

The cousins cheered again and I picked it up – very carefully – and carried it into the house. Mum was putting a stack of plates on the table – with a bottle of Dad's Special Elderflower Fizz.

'What about your next book, Caz?' she said, as she poured the Fizz. 'Have you started it yet?'

Aunt Caz looked puzzled. 'Didn't you hear what I said on TV?'

Mum shook her head. 'Our TV broke – just as you were starting. What did you say?'

'I told them about my next book.' Aunt Caz was bouncing with excitement. 'Beddington Potts is going to solve a mystery at a street-food festival. Isn't that a fantastic idea?'

A *street-food* festival? Why? For a moment that didn't make sense. Then I remembered. The books Aunt Caz wrote about Beddington Potts weren't just spy stories. They were spy stories *with RECIPES*.

Aunt Caz beamed. 'It's the perfect setting for a spy story! People from all over the world – cutthroat competition – secret recipes – a huge prize – it's got everything!'

'But . . . ' Aunt Dionne frowned. 'Do you know anything about street food?'

'I'm going to do research,' Aunt Caz said. 'By running a stall of my own – at a *real* food festival!'

Mum and Dad looked at each other. Aunt Caz was a terrible cook.

Aunt Caz laughed. 'Don't worry. I've got a great plan. And I've bought everything I need. I'll be off in the van – as soon as Ollie's set things up for me.'

I put the cake down on the table. 'What things?' I asked cautiously.

'The machine I bought with my prize money.' Aunt Caz was looking very excited.

'What *kind* of machine?' I said.

Aunt Caz beamed. 'It's a popcorn cannon!'

Chapter 3
The Popcorn Plan!

'A CANNON?' What was she talking about?

Aunt Caz laughed. 'It's a machine for making popcorn.'

'Yay!' Arabella pulled a chocolate moustache off the cake and stuck it on her face. 'Look, everyone! I'm Beddington Potts! And I'm going to make popcorn!'

All the other cousins copied her. While Mum cut the cake, they raced round the room in moustaches, shouting, 'No! *I'm* Beddington Potts!

I'm going to make popcorn!'

I stared at Aunt Caz. 'Why do you need a *machine*? You can make popcorn in the microwave.'

Aunt Caz rolled her eyes. 'But that's DULL, Ollie! Crowds won't come to see a *microwave*.'

'Crowds?' I said.

'Keep up, Ollie!' said Aunt Caz impatiently. 'That's what I'm going to sell on my stall. Popcorn – with amazing new flavours.'

I still didn't understand. 'Why do you need a stall? Can't you just go as a visitor?'

'That's *dull*,' Aunt Caz said firmly. 'If I'm one of the stallholders, I'll be able to get in with them, learn their secrets and share their troubles. That's why I've bought the cannon. I just need you to set it up, Ollie.'

Suddenly, everyone was nodding at me.

'Well?' said Aunt Caz. 'What are you waiting for, Ollie? Come and have a look at it!'

She headed outside and we all followed her and watched while Dad and Uncle Marek unloaded a heap of strange objects from the back of the van.

There was:

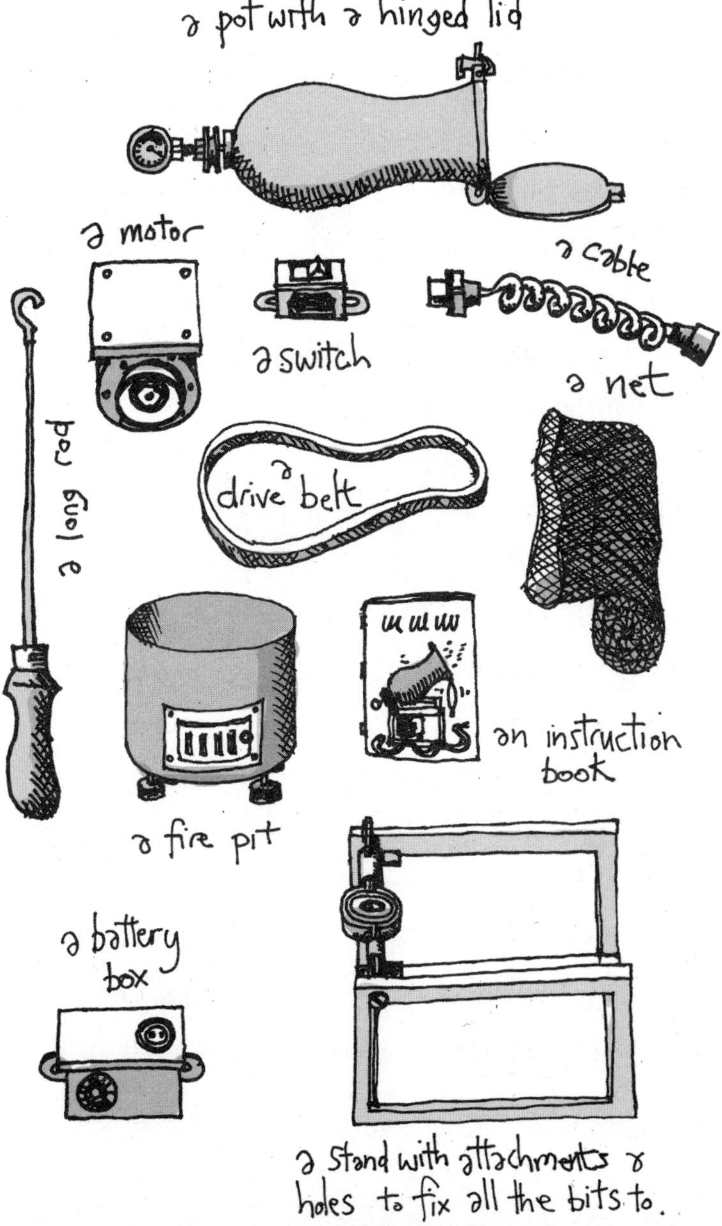

a pot with a hinged lid

a motor

a switch

a cable

a long pole

drive belt

a net

a fire pit

an instruction book

a battery box

a stand with attachments & holes to fix all the bits to.

We weren't the only people watching. Someone on the other side of the road had stopped to see what was going on.

A man in a grey coat with a camera hanging round his neck.

He was staring at the bits of the cannon. But he turned away quickly when he saw me looking at him. And no one else had noticed. They were all too busy clapping their hands and talking about popcorn.

'This is going to be the best thing in the festival!' Aunt Caz was saying. 'I'll make mountains of popcorn – with new, exciting flavours.' She waved at the instruction booklet. 'You just need to put it all together, Ollie! Now! Right here! Come on, get going!'

I looked down at the booklet. There was a big picture of the cannon on the front – with a firepit blazing underneath it. I wasn't going to set *that* up in the dark. Out in the street. With all the little cousins running around.

'It's too late now,' I said. 'I'll do it tomorrow. After school.'

Aunt Caz sighed and tapped her foot. 'That's too late. We have to *leave* then.'

I looked up at her. 'We?'

'You and me,' she said. As if that

was obvious. 'We'll leave straight after school, so we have the whole weekend at the festival.'

She'd just assumed I was going with her. But . . . I couldn't.

'I can't come this weekend,' I said. 'I'm camping out with Jin.'

Aunt Caz didn't even blink. 'So? Bring him too! The food festival's going to be *much* more fun than camping out in a wet tent. And you and Jin can work the cannon while I go round collecting material.'

'Material?' I said.

'For the next Beddington Potts adventure. *Concentrate*, Ollie!'

Aunt Caz was so excited she wasn't really listening. So I didn't waste time arguing. I would read the instructions for the popcorn cannon and put it together. And I'd tell her how to work it. But that was *all* I was going to do. I wasn't going to the food festival.

I was going to spend the weekend camping. With Jin.

Before I went to bed, I read the booklet three times. It still didn't seem very clear, so I searched on the computer – and found dozens of popcorn cannon videos.

They were terrifying!

I stared at the screen, watching one after another, over and over again. Watching people tipping corn into metal cannons, just like Aunt Caz's. They screwed up the door at the front of the cannon, then lit a fire in the firepit and pushed it underneath. The cannon got hotter and hotter and hotter – until the pressure inside was really high. Then the door was opened and . . .

WHOOOSH!

The popcorn exploded out, into a sack draped over the front of the cannon.

It was a clever idea. I understood exactly how it worked. But I kept imagining Aunt Caz doing the same thing. All on her own. By the time I went to bed, I was really worried.

'She won't *concentrate*,' I whispered to Gasket.

He stared up at me, looking puzzled.

I glanced round the room, to check my cousins were asleep, and then I whispered again.

'If Aunt Caz works the cannon on her own, she'll start the fire in the firepit. Then she'll think of something for Beddington Potts to do – and she'll start writing. And when she's writing, she forgets about everything else. So the pressure will go up and up, but she won't remember to move the firepit and open the door, so the pressure will *keep* going up until . . .'

I couldn't stop seeing the pictures in my head. If the cannon got too hot, the whole thing would explode, with flames and popcorn and bits of metal flying everywhere.

'There's going to be an accident,' I whispered.

Gasket licked my hand, but that didn't make me feel better. I lay down and stared up at the ceiling. I *really* wanted to go camping with Jin. I'd *promised.* But nothing would stop Aunt Caz using that cannon. Once she gets an idea in her head, she won't listen to anyone else.

If I wanted to keep her safe, I'd have to go to the food festival.

It was hours before I fell asleep. And when I did, I dreamed of giant explosions. Huge metal cannons shattering into pieces. Hot popcorn shooting every- where. Globs of gooey toffee flying through the air. And Aunt Caz shouting, 'Ollie! Fix it!'

My family think I can fix anything.

But I couldn't do it. Not in the dream. Every time I tried, the whole thing started again, with the cannon getting hotter and hotter and the pressure going up and up . . .

'No!' I yelled. 'NO-O-O!'

And then I wasn't dreaming any more. I was awake, standing on my bed and yelling 'NO!' at the top of my voice. I'd woken *everyone*. Dad was there. And Uncle Marek. And every single one of my cousins. They were all crowding round my bed, and the little ones were staring up at me, looking frightened.

'What's the matter, Ollie?' whispered Zak. 'Did you have a bad dream?'

I made myself smile. 'It's OK. I'm fine.'

But they still looked frightened. So I nodded at the alarm clock. 'Hey! It's *almost* time for breakfast. Shall I make some porridge?'

That stopped the cousins thinking about my dream. They grinned and started yelling.

'Yes! With raisins!'

'No, bananas!'

'Honey!'

'Raisins *and* bananas *and* honey *and* –'

They all ran downstairs ahead of me and I smiled at Dad – to show him I was OK – and then followed as fast as I could. I was going to need a *lot* of porridge.

But when we reached the kitchen . . . Aunt Caz was already there.

Chapter 5
Popcorn
Secrets

The top of the cooker was covered with saucepans, all bubbling away. And there were dozens of bowls on the worktops, all full of different things. Aunt Caz was tipping brown sugar into the food processor.

Gasket stopped in the doorway, sniffing warily.

'Aunt Caz, what are you *doing*?' I said.

'Inventing popcorn flavourings!' Aunt Caz turned round and beamed. 'Look!' She pointed at a list on the fridge door:

chilli & parsnips
chocolate and tomato
hot fudge, orange
pink candy floss
banoffee & ginger
double lemon fizz

'Aren't they fantastic?' she said. 'One of those is *sure* to win the Festival Prize!'

'There's a prize?' I said.

Aunt Caz's eyes gleamed. 'All the stalls are entered – and the prize is GIGANTIC! There'll probably be food spies everywhere, trying to steal the best recipes. But they won't get ours! We're going to be as clever as Beddington Potts. Master of Secrets! King of Concealment!'

'Could Beddington Potts –' *hide a popcorn cannon?* I

was going to say. But Aunt Caz didn't leave me time to speak. She just kept talking.

'There'll be REAL-LIFE SPYING. All around us. Isn't that great? I'll know what it *feels like* to be Beddington Potts!'

She waved her arms again – knocking three bowls off the worktop. I grabbed two of them and Gasket caught the other in his mouth. But Aunt Caz hardly noticed. She was much too excited.

'I'll keep all my flavourings in jars,' she said. 'Labelled in *code* – to stop people guessing what's inside. So come on, everyone – we're going on a hunt for empty jars! Whoever finds the most gets to *taste* everything I've made!'

She raced out of the kitchen – leaving the saucepans about to boil over – and all the cousins ran after her. I moved the saucepans and switched off the hob. Then I turned round. Through the window, I saw something odd on the other side of the road.

It was the man in the grey coat. Again. He still had

his camera – but now there was a long lens attached to the front. And it seemed to be pointing straight at our kitchen window.

As if he was taking a photograph of the kitchen. But why would he do that?

I looked round to see what would be in the picture – and there was Aunt Caz's list of popcorn flavourings, stuck up on the fridge. Exactly in line with the lens.

He's photographing the list, I thought for one wild moment. *He's a spy – stealing Aunt Caz's popcorn flavours!*

But then I looked back and the man had disappeared. There was nothing outside except the road and the houses opposite – and a couple of seagulls pecking around on the pavement. *I'm being ridiculous*, I thought. Our road wasn't the kind of place where exciting things happened.

Of course the man in the grey coat wasn't a spy. He was probably photographing the seagulls.

I forgot about him and started making a big pot of porridge – trying not to think about the food festival.

But I kept looking across at Aunt Caz's saucepans. Remembering how she'd left them boiling when she ran off to find the jars. If she did that with the cannon . . .

I sighed.

'It's no use,' I whispered to Gasket. 'We have to go with her. I'll tell Jin as soon as I get to school. He'll probably love the idea of going to a food festival.'

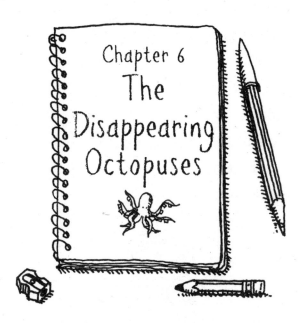

Chapter 6
The Disappearing Octopuses

I was right. Jin did love the idea – especially when I told him where the festival was.

'It's a brilliant place!' he said. 'There's a *coral reef*, Ollie. You'll be able to go snorkelling. And see fantastic sea creatures!'

'So will you.' I grinned. 'Aunt Caz says you can come too.'

Jin hesitated for a moment – and then shook his head.

'I can't. I *have* to camp. I've decided to do a Sleep-Out Challenge.'

'A *what*?'

'A Sleep-Out Challenge. To help solve the bluetop octopus mystery. I was reading about it last night and it's terrible what's happening. So I've set up a fund-raising page – look!' He held out his phone to show me.

'What mystery?' I said.

'Bluetop octopuses have suddenly started disappearing. And no one knows why. So I'm going to raise a thousand pounds for Free the Sea!' Jin scrolled down the page, to show me. 'To help their scientists find out.'

'I've never even *heard* of bluetop octopuses,' I said.

Jin sighed impatiently. He always knows about things like that. 'They're *totally amazing creatures*. They can solve puzzles and open locked boxes and unscrew jars and use tools and . . .'

He kept on talking. Faster and faster and faster.

'. . . no one knows why they're vanishing. Some people think it's conger eels – because they eat octo-puses – but no one actually knows, so it needs loads of research . . .'

When Jin gets a new interest, it's all he can think about. Ten minutes later, he was still telling me facts about the bluetop octopus. And could see why

he wanted to save them. They *were* amazing. But I couldn't concentrate on octopuses. I needed to make him understand why I couldn't do the sleep-out too.

I pulled the instruction booklet out of my pocket. 'Look,' I said. 'Aunt Caz has bought one of these.'

Jin stared at the picture on the front. 'A *popcorn cannon*?'

I nodded. 'She's taking it to the food festival. I'm worried she'll light the burner and then start writing and . . .'

Jin nodded. He's known my family all his life, and I didn't need to explain any more. 'You have to go with her,' he said. 'Don't worry about me. I'll be camping out for weeks and weeks, so you can join in later. I won't give up, because it's really important to find out . . .'

And he went back to talking about bluetop octopuses.

I tried to listen, but my mind kept going back to the food festival. And the popcorn cannon.

I had to make sure it was safe.

Chapter 7
Off to the Food Festival!

Aunt Caz wasn't joking when she said we were leaving *straight after school*. The van was there, right by the gate, when Jin and I walked out of the building that afternoon. I could hear Gasket barking in the back.

Aunt Caz started hooting – as if she thought we might not notice her.

'Looks like you're leaving right now!' Jin said. He grinned. 'Have a great time.'

'You too.' I grinned back. 'Hope it doesn't rain on your tent.'

There was no time to say anything else. Aunt Caz was calling me.

'OLLIE!'

I gave Jin a wave and climbed into the van. 'Aren't we going home first?'

Aunt Caz shook her head. 'I've brought your things. *And* your tool belt – in case anything needs fixing.' I sat down and she dumped a huge pile of papers on to my lap.

'You'd better do that,' she said. 'While we're on the way.'

I looked down at the papers. 'Do what?'

'Work out what we need to charge for the popcorn.' Aunt Caz revved the engine and the van shot away from the kerb.

'But –'

'I've given you the bills, so you can see what I've paid. Just work out a sensible price – but not too expensive, because we want lots of people to buy the popcorn and LOVE it, so we win the Super Snack Competition –'

'But –'

'– and when you've done that, we need four big posters, to go all round the van, so people can't miss them.'

'But what shall I –'

'Ollie! I can't do *everything*! If you sort out the prices and the posters, I can concentrate on –'

SCREECH!

We'd reached a red light. Aunt Caz slammed on the brakes, just in time.

'OK,' I said quickly. 'You concentrate on driving.' I started looking through the bills she'd given me. They were in a terrible muddle – and every time

Aunt Caz braked, they all slithered on to the floor. It took me *hours* to write down all the payments. And then add them up. And then work out how much popcorn each bag would hold, and how much profit we ought to make, and what each bag should cost . . .

I kept getting interrupted by nudges from Gasket and messages from Jin. Every time that happened, I lost my place and had to start again. I was *finally* getting to the end of the last long sum, when I suddenly heard a lot of shouting ahead. Aunt Caz started driving *very* slowly, Gasket put his nose on my knee . . .

. . . and I smelt the sea.

Chapter 8
The Festival Ferry

It was almost dark. Looking up, I saw a long stone jetty ahead of us. There was a car ferry at the far end, and beyond it, away on the horizon, the setting sun laid a path of gold across the deep-blue water.

Aunt Caz steered the van on to the jetty.

'We're going on a *boat*?' I said.

'Of course we're going on a boat.' Aunt Caz shook her head, as if I was being stupid. 'How else could we get to the island?'

She drove on to the ferry, with half a dozen sailors shouting instructions, and parked the van right in the middle of the car deck.

I looked out of the window. All around us were other vans, painted with names in bright colours.

PATRICIA'S PERFECT PIZZA
THE ULTIMATE BBQ
CAKE AND COFFEE HEAVEN
JOE'S JACKETS
– 15 DIFFERENT FILLINGS

I gave Gasket a pat. 'It's going to be great!' I said. 'Hope we get a chance to try all the food.'

Aunt Caz turned off the engine, opened her door and jumped out of the van. 'You see?' She waved her arms at all the other vans. 'Isn't it stupendous? And the most stupendous thing of all will be *our popcorn*! We're going to win that prize, Ollie!'

She started running up the stairs to the main deck. I could hear lots of noise coming from above us. Talking and laughing. Even some singing. I let Gasket out of the van and turned round to lock it.

'Sounds as if they're having fun upstairs,' I said.

But when I turned round, Gasket wasn't there. He was halfway across the car deck, sniffing excitedly at one van after another. Of course! They must all be full of exotic foods and strange spices. He had a whole world of new smells to explore.

I let him enjoy it for a few moments. Then I called, 'Come on, boy! Let's go and meet the other stallholders.' We went up the stairs and found ourselves in a big passenger lounge crowded with people drinking coffee and chatting to each other. It was obvious they were all going to the festival. And the walls of the lounge were plastered with posters advertising it.

THE ISLAND OF SNACKS!

HOLIDAY IN STREET FOOD HEAVEN!!!

TOURISM FOR YOUR TASTE BUDS!!!!

The people were advertising too. Most of them were wearing T-shirts that said things like:

SPICE UP YOUR LIFE WITH FLORA'S FRITTERS

DUNK OUR DELICIOUS DOUGHNUTS!

IT'S ALWAYS HOT ENOUGH FOR ICE CREAM

Aunt Caz had already made friends. She was in the middle of a cluster of people – all talking about one thing.

Food!

Snippets of conversation came floating towards me. '. . . added extra chilli . . .' '. . . sure to win!' '. . . my granny's special recipe . . .' '. . . three new flavours since last year . . .'

Aunt Caz waved at me. 'Come on, Ollie! I've got you some hot chocolate and a bagel. And a bagel for Gasket too.'

I went across to take them, and the adults around her nodded hello. Then they went back to talking at each other. But there were a couple of kids on the edge of the crowd. A boy and a girl. They smiled and made room for me.

'Hi,' they said together.

I blinked. 'You're twins!'

Chapter 9
The Twins

The girl laughed. 'Why does everyone *tell* us?'

'We *know* we're twins,' said the boy.

I looked at their T-shirts. They were bright green and across the front they said: NED AND NORA'S NOODLES – THE FESTIVAL'S BEST!

'So you're Nora,' I said to the girl. 'And this is Ned? Right?'

The boy shook his head. 'I'm Sam and this is Daisy. Ned and Nora are our mum and dad. They've sold noodles at the festival for twenty years.'

'All their friends have stalls too,' Daisy said. 'Belinda's ice-cream cones –'

'Mr George's cheese fritters –' said Sam.

'Mrs Simpson's stuffed cucumbers –'

'Frederico's toasted bagels –'

They were both grinning. I grinned back at them and looked round for two more bright green T-shirts. But I couldn't see any.

'So do you live on the island?' I asked.

The twins stopped smiling.

'We *used* to live there,' said Sam. 'Until last year. Mum and Dad ran the Duchess's Zoo and it was a lovely, happy zoo. With lots of things for the animals to do – and great views out across the sea to the coral reef.'

'We used to go snorkelling every day,' Daisy said. 'But after last year's festival –' She stopped suddenly, as if she might burst into tears.

Sam was frowning. 'The moment last year's festival ended, the Duchess sacked Mum and Dad. For

no reason. She closed the zoo and started making all kinds of changes.'

'It's *horrible*,' Daisy muttered. 'So Mum and Dad left the island and couldn't bear to come back for the festival.'

'But *you've* come,' I said.

Sam looked fierce. 'It wouldn't be a proper food festival without Ned and Nora's Noodles. So we told Mum and Dad we'd run the stall instead.'

Daisy nodded. 'Dad's friend Joe is bringing his caravan for us to use. So all we have to do is set up – and start cooking.'

'Good luck!' I said. 'I hope you win the festival prize.' I knew Aunt Caz wanted it – but maybe these two needed it more.

Sam nodded. 'That would be great. But the main thing is – we want to sell *lots* of noodles.'

'We're going to break Mum and Dad's record!' Daisy said.

I was going to ask what the record was. But before I could say anything else, Aunt Caz turned round and called to me.

'Come on, Ollie! Let's go out on deck. I want to watch for the island!'

'I'll just get some water for Gasket,' I called back. I gave Sam and Daisy a grin. 'See you later! Can't wait to try your noodles!'

They smiled and waved goodbye as I went up to the counter.

When I asked for water, the man behind the counter poured some into a bowl. 'Lovely dog,' he said, nodding down at Gasket. 'Bringing him to the festival?'

I nodded. 'We've got a stall. My aunt wants to win the prize.'

The man shook his head. 'Better watch out for the Duchess then. She's set her heart on winning this year. And when she really wants something . . .' He pulled a face. 'She's a very determined woman. Stops at nothing to get what she wants.'

I grinned. 'Aunt Caz is determined too. Who's –'

Who's the Duchess? I was going to ask, but the man turned away to serve someone else, so I picked up the bowl and followed Aunt Caz outside. She was at the front of the boat, staring ahead.

'Look, Ollie!' she called. 'There's the island!' We were getting really close.

I stood beside her and gave Gasket the water. The island was blazing with light. All the buildings round the harbour were strung with fairy lights and huge floodlights made the streets as bright as day. As we sailed closer, I could even read the posters on the walls.

WELCOME TO THE WORLD'S GREATEST FOOD FESTIVAL!
SAMPLE THE SNACKS!!
WHO WILL WIN THE PRIZE???

There was a brass band playing on one side of the harbour and a jazz orchestra on the other side. People were bustling about, setting up stalls – and

seagulls were circling overhead, looking for food to scavenge.

I leaned over the rail and took a picture to send to Jin.

Wish you were here???

I pushed the phone back into my pocket, without waiting for an answer. The ferry was moving towards the quay and I didn't want to miss anything.

Even from where we were, everything smelt *fantastic*. There were so many different smells I couldn't keep track of them all. I glanced down at Gasket, to check it wasn't too much for him.

But he wasn't looking at me. He was staring along the deck, at someone coming out of the passenger lounge.

The man in the grey coat.

Chapter 10
The Duchess

Was it *really* him? The man I'd seen outside our kitchen window? It was hard to be sure. When he saw me looking, he shot back into the lounge, as if he didn't want to be seen.

But if it *was* him . . . he must be going to the festival. So maybe he *had* been trying to steal Aunt Caz's recipes?

Maybe he really was a spy!

I stared at the lounge door. Should I follow him, to

get another look? Or would that be dangerous? I was still trying to make up my mind when there was a burst of noise from the shore. A sudden, loud fanfare.

I turned round and saw three trumpeters in purple coats, marching into the big square next to the quay.

Behind the trumpeters, driven very slowly, came a big purple car with its headlights blazing. It had purple upholstery and a chauffeur at the wheel. He was in purple too.

In the back of the car was a woman in a GIGANTIC purple hat, decorated with peacock feathers.

'It's the Duchess!' squealed Aunt Caz.

The car pulled up under the floodlights. All around us on the boat, passengers were whispering and pointing. And there were shouts coming from the shore. Everyone was staring at the Duchess.

Except Gasket. He started growling softly.

'What's the matter?' I whispered. 'Don't you like the trumpets?'

Then I saw that he wasn't watching the trumpeters.

He was looking at something else. Something that

was lumbering along behind the Duchess's car.

A huge elephant.

It was walking very slowly, with its head down and its feet dragging, pulling a cart full of striped material, trimmed with glittering fringes and strings of golden bells.

'The Duchess has an *elephant*?' I said.

'Didn't you know?' said one of the sailors. 'She's obsessed with animals.'

'Got her own private zoo,' said another. 'Lions and tigers and everything.'

'And little dogs,' said the first sailor. 'Look, she's got some in the car now.'

He pointed and I saw three miniature poodles squashed in beside the Duchess. They peered at the crowd as if they wanted to be out there, not shut up in a stuffy car. The car stopped beside a big white

marquee and the Duchess beckoned to the elephant.
It plodded slowly into the big square and a team of
workers leaped forward and started unloading the
striped material.

It was a huge awning.

The workers started putting it up at one end of
the marquee. As they worked, the Duchess's voice
boomed out of the big loudspeakers round the harbour. 'Welcome, stallholders! You are going to be
part of the greatest street-food festival in the world!'

The trumpeters played another fanfare. Then the
Duchess spoke again.

'Be ready for the Grand Opening at eight tomorrow morning. We're expecting lots of hungry tourists.
And don't forget to try the food yourselves –' the

Duchess waved a hand at the awning going up behind her – 'especially my Amazing Knitted Noodles!'

She lifted something else out of her bag – and her image was instantly projected on to the side of the big white marquee. In her hand, she was dangling something that looked like a short striped scarf.

Could it be the knitted noodles?

Could you *do* that with noodles?

The Duchess held it up, so the camera would get a clear picture. It was definitely knitting. The image on

the marquee was so big I could see all the little loops.

But was it *food*?

As if the Duchess had read my mind, she held out the noodle scarf, nodding to her little dogs.

They looked back at her for a moment, as if they were scared of making a mistake. Then the Duchess nodded and one opened its mouth, took three quick bites and ate every scrap of the noodles.

TA-DA! The trumpeters played another fanfare. The Duchess looked round at the marquee workers

and they all cheered mechanically. As if someone had pressed a switch.

Then the Duchess's car turned around and drove slowly back the way it had come, with the elephant plodding behind, pulling the empty cart.

I looked down at Gasket. He was standing stiffly, with his ears back, staring at the Duchess's car.

'What's up?' I said.

Before I had a chance to guess what he was thinking, Aunt Caz was tugging at my sleeve.

'Come on! You heard the Duchess. We have to be ready by eight tomorrow morning. We need to get off this boat and find our place!'

Gasket and I followed her back to the van, but I wasn't thinking about our stall. I was too busy thinking about those noodles. They really were *knitted*!

But how?

Chapter 11
The Noodle Puzzle

Noodles are really, *really* slippery. If you tried to knit them by hand, they'd just fall off the needles, wouldn't they? Over and over again. So just that strip the Duchess had fed to the poodle would have taken hours and hours to make – with the noodles slithering everywhere.

But if she was taking *hours* to knit them, surely they'd dry out? And get brittle? So the strip would never *get* finished. Because the noodles would all start snapping.

So how *had* she done it?

Had she got some kind of noodle-knitting machine? That might be able to knit faster. But she'd still have to stop the noodles drying out. Maybe . . . an underwater machine?

But electricity was really dangerous underwater. And steam engines and petrol engines wouldn't work. So how . . . ?

I was still trying to puzzle it out as Aunt Caz drove off the ferry. She pulled a map out of her pocket and dropped it into my lap.

'That shows where we have to park,' she said. 'Every stall has a special place.'

I unfolded the paper and studied the map. We obviously weren't going to be in the big square with the Duchess's marquee. That was already full. And the streets nearest the harbour were jammed with stalls too.

'We need to go down that little side street,' I said. 'And then turn left at the end.'

Aunt Caz spun the wheel and the van squealed

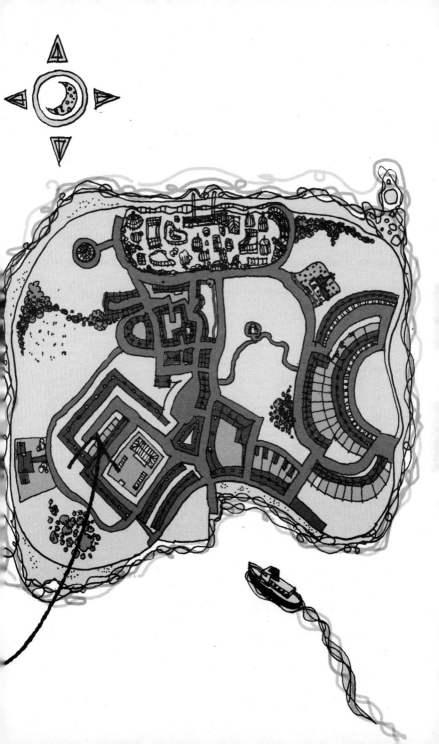

round the corner. The little street was lined with stalls on both sides. There was just room to drive between them. As we turned right, she jammed on the brakes.

'It's not a very good place,' she said crossly. 'We're a long way from the main square.'

We'd driven into a short dead-end road, which only had room for a couple of stalls. I pointed to a space on the left.

'We're next to that green caravan.'

Aunt Caz edged into the space. Then she turned off the engine and opened her door. 'Come on then. Let's set up!'

I stopped thinking about noodles and knitting. It was time to concentrate on the cannon now. By the time I got to the back of the van, Aunt Caz had already opened the boot. I looked in – and blinked.

'Where's the quad bike?' I said. It should have been in the van, hanging on the brackets I'd fitted to hold it. Instead, there was just the cannon – and boxes and boxes of *Beddington Potts* books.

Aunt Caz shrugged. 'We won't need the bike. And I wanted the space for my books.'

'Books?' I said. 'At a food festival?'

'I'm going to sell them next to the popcorn. People need something to read while they're eating.' Aunt Caz waved her hand impatiently. 'Stop *chattering*, Ollie. Let's get the cannon out. Shall we put it here, in the middle of the road? Then people are sure to notice it.'

'No!' I shook my head. Very hard. 'We need a

really safe place, where no one can get near the fire.'
I took a step back and looked round. 'Maybe . . . it
could go between us and the caravan? If they don't
mind.'

'Go and ask them!' Aunt Caz said. 'Promise them
free popcorn if they say yes!'

I went over to the green caravan, Gasket trotting
behind me. There was an awning in front of it. Their
stall wasn't set up yet, but I could smell something
delicious cooking inside. I knocked on the door and
called out, 'Hello! I'm Ollie and this is Gasket. Can
we ask you something?'

There was a little pause and then the door opened

slowly. 'Hello,' said a gloomy voice.

'Are *you* selling noodles too?' said another one. Even gloomier.

That was when I noticed the words on the side of the caravan: NED AND NORA'S NOODLES.

'Sam?' I said. 'Daisy? It's me.'

Chapter 12

Sam and Daisy

It was Sam and Daisy all right – but they looked quite different now. When I'd left them on the boat, they'd been cheerful and excited – determined to sell lots of noodles. Now Sam was frowning and Daisy looked anxious and upset.

'What's the matter?' I said. 'Is something wrong?'

Sam gave a short, unhappy laugh. 'You mean – apart from being stuck in this dead end? With the Duchess selling *her* noodles in the main square?'

For a second I didn't get it. Then I realized. 'You're afraid people will buy her noodles – instead of yours?'

Daisy nodded sadly. 'She's grabbed the best place for her stall. Joe tried to get a good place for ours, but they made him park the caravan down here.'

'People might not even *come* down this street,' Sam said. 'And even if they do, they'll probably be full of noodles already.'

'We might not sell *any* of ours,' said Daisy.

They looked wretched. How could I cheer them up?

'Look, the knitted noodles are fun,' I said. 'But they must take *hours* to make. Maybe they even need a special machine. And all that costs money. So they're going to be *really expensive.*'

Daisy sniffed and wiped her eyes. 'You mean . . . ours will be better value?'

I nodded. 'They're bound to be. And I bet they taste better too.'

A tiny smile flitted across Sam's face. 'Dad makes

the noodles himself. He's got a secret recipe.'

'They're *scrumptious*!' said Daisy.

I nodded. 'There you are then.'

But the twins still weren't happy. 'No one's going to *know* they're scrumptious,' said Daisy, 'unless they find our stall. And that's not going to happen, is it? Not while we're stuck away down here.'

For a second, I thought she could be right. Then I realized – I had the answer to that!

'Of course they'll find it!' I said. 'When they come to see our cannon!'

Chapter 13
Publicity!

Sam blinked. 'Your – *what?*'

I grinned. 'We've got a popcorn cannon. It's really exciting. Everyone's going to be talking about it – so people will come flocking down here. This street will be full!'

'So . . . they'll notice our stall too?' Sam's eyes gleamed.

'We'll make sure they do!' Daisy dived into the caravan and came back with a brush and a pot of paint. 'We're going to *advertise*!'

She and Sam put their heads together, chattering excitedly, and I hurried back to Aunt Caz. She'd left the cannon for me to sort out and had started sticking posters on the van. Not the little posters I'd made on the way. Mine just said:

Fresh popcorn

Lots of delicious flavours

Aunt Caz was sticking up huge sheets of paper and covering them with gigantic coloured letters.

BEDDINGTON POPS!
SPY OUR EXCITING POPCORN!
INVESTIGATE OUR FAMOUS FLAVOURS!

Sam and Daisy were putting up new signs too.

NED AND NORA'S FAMOUS NOODLES!
TOTALLY DELICIOUS!!
REALLY GOOD VALUE!!!

Aunt Caz lifted a table out of the van and set it up in the road. She heaped the Beddington Potts books on top of it and added another sign.

81

EAT THE POPCORN – BUY THE BOOK!

Then she looked round at me. 'You need to get the cannon going, Ollie! Or there won't *be* any popcorn to sell.'

She was right. I couldn't put it off any longer. I went to the back of the van and started lifting everything out. I put the parts as far back as I could, where no one was going to walk. Then I took a deep breath.

When I'm fixing a new machine, I like to be somewhere quiet. On my own. With time to make sure I follow the instructions in order. But there was no chance of that now. Sam and Daisy came across to watch, other people were drifting down the street to see what was happening, and Aunt Caz was jumping up and down with excitement.

'Just wait till you see!' she kept saying to everyone. 'This is brilliant!'

Only Gasket knew how I was feeling. He sat beside me, very quietly, while I re-read the instruction booklet. When I'd finished, just to be sure I had everything right, I decided to test it. I filled the

cannon with corn, screwed on its lid and fitted it on to the stand.

Then I reached for the firepit.

'This is the dangerous part,' I said loudly. 'Keep back, everyone!'

I got the fire going and when it was blazing hot, I pushed the firepit into place and switched on the motor that kept the cannon turning.

'What happens next?' Aunt Caz said impatiently. 'Shall I fetch the flavourings?'

I shook my head and concentrated on the pressure gauge, watching it go up and up and up, while my heart thumped faster and faster and faster . . .

And then it was time! I pulled the firepit away into a safe corner, fitted the long, cylindrical bag over the mouth of the cannon, used the rod to undo the lid and . . .

WHOOOSH!

The corn exploded out into the bag and everyone screamed with excitement.

'Well done, Ollie!' Aunt Caz shrieked. 'Now we're ready for the festival!'

She grabbed the popcorn bag and raced off to try out her flavourings. Everyone else wandered off, chattering excitedly about the cannon – and I was left to deal with the fire.

I put it out and then looked down at Gasket. 'We were right to come, weren't we? Aunt Caz just went off and left it burning.'

Gasket stood up and wagged his tail. I could see he understood. I'd made the right decision – even though it meant leaving Jin to camp on his own. I hoped he was OK.

I took out my phone to have a quick look at his fundraising page – and he'd already raised *over a thousand pounds*. Fantastic! I messaged him straight away.

£1k! Well done!!!

The answer came back at once.

> They'll need a lot more if they're going to save the bluetop octopus

He sent a picture too – the entrance of his tent, rain dripping down outside. I patted Gasket's head as he flopped down on my legs.

'Bet Jin wishes he had someone like you,' I said.

It looked cold and miserable inside that tent. But I knew Jin wouldn't give up, however awful it was. If he thinks something's right, he *never* gives up.

I sent him a thumbs up and went to help Aunt Caz. We needed to bag up all the popcorn before we went to bed.

Chapter 14
A Taste of
Noodles

At least Jin could lie in the next morning. No such luck for us. We were woken at 5 a.m. – by trumpets!

There's some mistake, I thought when I looked at the time. But there wasn't. Aunt Caz was already heading for the shower.

'Hurry up!' she shouted over her shoulder. 'We need to get working. I want that cannon ready to pop more corn – BANG on eight o'clock!'

She laughed at her own joke. But I was too hungry to laugh.

'What about breakfast?' I said. Very loudly, because the shower had started up.

'I've had a great idea about that!' Aunt Caz yelled back. 'The Duchess's stall is opening early. We'll get some of her noodles. I can't wait to see what they're like. I'll get some for Sam and Daisy too.'

'That's *rude*!' I shouted. 'We ought to be eating theirs.'

But Aunt Caz wasn't listening. When she gets an idea in her head, that's IT. Ten minutes later, showered and dressed, she was charging down the road to the Duchess's marquee.

She came back with four bags of noodle strips, all different colours. On the way to the van, she banged

on Sam and Daisy's door.

'Breakfast!' she shouted.

Sam opened the door and Daisy peered over his shoulder. They looked very tired, as though they'd been working all night. Aunt Caz waved the bag of noodle strips at them.

'Thought you'd like to try these,' she said. 'Come and have breakfast with us.'

They looked at each other and nodded. Jumping out of their caravan, they followed Aunt Caz and we all squeezed round the table in our van.

Aunt Caz tipped the noodle strips on to a plate. 'Eat up!' she said. 'We're going to need all the energy we can get.'

I picked up a strip and bit into it. The first strip was delicious – but what did it taste of? Strawberries? Oranges? I couldn't quite make up my mind. And the second one . . . ?

I was still trying to decide, when Aunt Caz gave an angry shout.

'Banoffee and ginger!'

'What?' I blinked at her.

Daisy stared, and Sam almost dropped his noodles.

Aunt Caz had just tasted her first strip – and she was furious. She shook the noodles at us. 'That bit tastes of banoffee and ginger! And this one –' she took a bite of the second strip '– that's double lemon fizz!' She was so angry I thought she was going to choke.

Sam and Daisy looked at each other. Then they took a bite of their own noodles – and looked at each other.

'These are just like *Dad's noodles*!' whispered Daisy. 'The way they've soaked up the sauce –'

'– and stayed soft, without drying out.' Sam nodded. 'Someone's using his secret recipe!'

But . . . that had to be impossible. Their Dad's secret noodles *and* Aunt Caz's secret flavourings? 'It must be a coincidence,' I said.

Aunt Caz almost exploded. 'A COINCIDENCE?' she spluttered. 'Do you think I don't know my own flavourings? I *invented* them, Ollie!'

'And Dad invented these noodles.' Sam said. 'When they're put into hot sauce, they absorb it. So they're super-tasty and they don't go hard and brittle.'

Aunt Caz bit into her third noodle strip – and turned purple with rage. 'Hot fudge and orange!' she spluttered. 'Don't tell me *that's* a coincidence, Ollie. I've been robbed!'

'So have we!' Daisy whispered. 'Someone's stolen Dad's secret.'

Aunt Caz jumped up, sending noodles flying everywhere. 'Call the police!' she yelled.

'Wait! Please!' I held up my hands to stop her charging out of the van. 'Remember – they're the *Duchess's* noodles.'

'So?' Aunt Caz looked impatient. 'What difference does that make?'

'Remember that huge purple car?' I said. 'And the elephant, and the trumpeters? The Duchess is *in charge* round here. It looks as if everyone does what she wants. So we need some real evidence if we're going to the police.'

Aunt Caz almost exploded. 'We've *got* the evidence. All the police need to do is taste the noodles!'

'That won't prove anything.' I turned to Sam and Daisy. '*You* can see that, can't you? We've only just arrived on the island. No one's had time to steal –'

And then I remembered the man in the grey coat.

Chapter 15

Real Spies!

Of course! He hadn't waited till we reached the island. He'd tracked us down at home – and photographed Aunt Caz's list *to see what she was planning.*

Aunt Caz was watching my face. 'What is it, Ollie?'

I knew she'd go wild if I told her what I'd seen. I had to be *sure* before I said anything, so I looked at Sam and Daisy. 'Did you see anyone strange hanging round your house?' I said. 'While you were getting ready for the festival?'

Sam started shaking his head – but Daisy nudged him. 'No, there *was* someone!' she said. 'That woman with the terrier. Don't you remember?'

For a second, Sam looked puzzled. Then his mouth dropped open. 'You mean the one who knocked on the door? And asked you for a glass of water?'

Daisy nodded. 'Her dog raced in before I could stop him. Remember? And Dad was really annoyed about being interrupted, *because he was telling us how to make the noodles –*'

'– but the woman kept chasing the dog,' Sam said slowly. 'And when it went behind the fridge – *she reached round to shoo it out.* Do you think –'

'– she stuck a bug on the back of the fridge?' Daisy nodded thoughtfully. 'I bet that's what she was doing.'

'You see?' Aunt Caz said triumphantly. 'I was right! That woman was a spy! She stole Sam and Daisy's recipe. And she must have stolen mine too. Did you see her, Ollie?'

I shook my head. 'No – but I saw a man outside our

house. He was taking pictures through the window.'

Aunt Caz's eyes opened wide. 'The *kitchen* window?'

I nodded. 'It seemed a bit weird, but I couldn't believe he was really a spy. Not till I saw him again. On the ferry.'

'Then you *knew*!' Aunt Caz was almost smiling. 'You know what that means, don't you, Ollie? We're in the middle of a *real-life mystery*!'

I'd never seen her look so excited.

'It's only a guess,' I said carefully.

'No! It *must* be true!' Aunt Caz's eyes lit up. 'There are *real spies* on this island. People like Beddington Potts. With a trained spy dog too! I can do some *fantastic* research!'

Sam and Daisy looked baffled. They had no idea what she meant, of course. But I hadn't got time to explain.

'Aunt Caz,' I said, 'you mustn't –'

But she wasn't listening. She'd started opening cupboards and pulling out clothes. 'I need a disguise,' she muttered. 'So I can track them to their lair.'

'NO!' I grabbed one of her arms. 'They might be dangerous!'

'That's right!' said Sam. And Daisy nodded as hard as she could.

But Aunt Caz didn't take any notice. 'Writers have to take risks!' she said. And then – 'Aha! That's what I want!'

She pulled out a big hat and a pair of dark glasses.

When she'd put them on, she dragged the cover off my bed and wrapped it round her shoulders, like a cloak.

'No one will recognize me now!' she said, heading for the door.

'Look –' I thought fast, trying to calm her down. 'You have to be like Beddington Potts. Sharper than a needle!'

That stopped her. 'What do you mean?' she said.

'Well, he . . . he wouldn't just go charging off, would he? He's really clever – so he'd think everything through first. And make a *plan*.'

Aunt Caz stood in the doorway, frowning. 'How can I make a plan until I track them down?'

'It'll be too late then.' I tried to sound calm. 'There won't be time to think, so you'll need to know exactly . . .'

She was definitely hesitating. I just needed a few more minutes. But before I could say anything else –

TA-RA! TA-RA! TA-RA-DI-RA-DI-RAAAAA!

A huge trumpet fanfare sounded from the main square.

Aunt Caz blinked. 'What's that?'

'It's the Festival opening,' Sam said. 'It's just about to start. The Duchess –'

Aunt Caz didn't wait to hear the rest. '*Everyone's*

going to be at the opening! It's the perfect chance to go spy-spotting!'

Before anyone else could speak, she jumped out of the van and strode off towards the square.

Chapter 16
The Opening

Sam grabbed Daisy's hand. 'She's right!' he said. 'Let's go and see if we can spot the woman with the terrier. Come on!'

They dashed off after Aunt Caz. And I looked down at Gasket.

'We'd better follow them,' I said. I had to try and keep Aunt Caz out of trouble. When she got excited she always forgot to be careful. She hadn't even remembered about locking the van.

I took the keys out of the ignition and locked the door behind us. Then Gasket and I ran after the others. But we were too late to catch up with them. The streets were crowded with people, all heading for the square.

By the time we arrived, it was jammed full. Aunt Caz had pushed forward, towards the Duchess's marquee. She was standing right by the stage – next to the Duchess's elephant – and when she saw me, she stood on tiptoe and waved. But there was no way I could reach her.

The trumpeters blew another fanfare and the Duchess climbed on to the stage. She was dressed in plum-coloured robes, with a jewelled dagger hanging from her belt. Her little dogs were behind her, on leads. They were struggling to get away, but she dragged them on to the stage.

With a regal wave, she walked up to a yellow ribbon stretched across the stage. Pulling the dagger out of her belt, she flourished it in the air.

'Welcome!' she said.

Her image was projected on to the marquee behind her, huge and purple, with the dagger gleaming in her hand. She lifted it up, high above the yellow ribbon . . .

. . . and that was when I saw the man in the grey coat.

He was standing a few people along from Aunt Caz, staring up at the stage as if he was an ordinary person. But spies were like that, weren't they? What was it Aunt Caz always said? *When Beddington Potts wants to hide, he just blends into the crowd.* That's what this man was doing.

He was so busy being ordinary that he didn't see me staring at him. But Aunt Caz did. She turned to wave at me – and then followed my eyes, to see what I was looking at. When she spotted the grey coat, a big smile spread across her face. She edged through the crowd until she was standing right next to the man. Then she looked back at me again – and winked.

No! I thought. *No!* I knew what that wink meant. When the spy left the square, she was going to follow him. That meant she was probably walking into danger. What could I do? I couldn't get through to her, because of the crowd. And if I shouted from where I was, the spy was sure to spot her and that might be dangerous.

But I couldn't let her follow him on her own.

There was only one thing to do. I crouched down and whispered to Gasket. 'Go to Aunt Caz.'

He gave me a puzzled look.

'Aunt Caz,' I whispered again. 'Stay with Aunt Caz. Go on, boy.'

He stared at me for a couple of seconds and then wagged his tail and disappeared into the forest of legs in front of us. It felt strange, watching him go, but I could tell he'd understood. A few seconds later, he appeared right next to Aunt Caz.

Just as the Duchess started to speak.

She brandished her dagger again and beamed down at the crowd. 'Welcome to our Grand Festival! For the next two days, our streets will be full of delicious food. Enjoy all the wonderful snacks – especially my sensational Knitted Noodles!'

The trumpets blared and the Duchess raised her dagger high into the air. 'I now declare this Festival open!' she shouted.

I have to take a video for Jin! I thought. I pulled out my phone just in time, as the Duchess swung the dagger in a great arc and brought it down on the shiny ribbon. The ribbon fell apart and the striped cat lifted its head and gave a small, tired roar.

Got it! I thought. Then I looked back at Aunt Caz – but she'd vanished. And so had the man in the grey coat.

I couldn't see Gasket either. Which was good, of course, because it meant he'd followed Aunt Caz – but it felt strange walking back to the van without him.

Chapter 17
Trouble

To cheer myself up, I sent the video of the opening to
Jin – with a quick message underneath.

> No time for snorkelling yet. Hope
> you got more sleep than I did!

The answer came straight away.
– and then a photo of his tent, tangled up in a tree.

It was the most miserable message I'd ever seen.
I replied as fast as I could:

> Hope it's better tonight!

> Don't think I can stand another night 😔

What? That didn't sound like Jin. He must be feeling really, *really* miserable. How could I cheer him up?

I was trying to think, when Sam and Daisy came racing past me, on their way back from the square.

'What are you doing?' shouted Sam. 'You need to get your cannon going again!'

'All Mum and Dad's friends are talking about it!' Daisy yelled. 'And they're on their way NOW!'

'I'm coming!' I said. 'Just a couple of seconds.' I couldn't go without answering Jin. Quickly I typed a message.

> You can't give up! Think of the bluetop octopuses! You're doing really well – and the octopuses NEED that money!! Keep going!!!

I sent it as fast as I could, then pushed my phone into my pocket and ran after Sam and Daisy. By the time I got there, they'd opened their stall and there was a delicious smell of noodle sauce drifting up the road. All we needed now was the cannon!

I started the fire in the firepit and filled the cannon with corn. Then I shut the lid and pushed the firepit underneath.

Just in time! A couple of minutes later, people started wandering down our little side street. They looked a bit doubtful, as if they weren't sure what to expect.

'It's here!' I shouted. 'It's heating up! Come and watch it explode!'

'And while you're waiting – snack on our noodles!' called Daisy. 'Hot and tasty!'

By the time the cannon was ready, the street was crowded with people eating noodles and staring at the cannon. I checked the pressure gauge and made sure everyone was far enough away.

'Here we go!' I shouted. 'STAND CLEAR!'

Then I fitted the bag on to the end of the cannon, pulled the firepit away and opened the door.

People cheered and laughed – and bought lots of popcorn. They went away chattering, obviously longing to tell everyone else about the cannon.

'It's going to be a busy day!' I called to Sam and Daisy.

Daisy nodded and Sam gave me a thumbs up. They were both looking very happy.

We did it all over again. And again. And again. By the end of the morning, I'd sold a mountain of popcorn. And Sam and Daisy had actually run out of noodles. They had to make some more – which meant people saw them stretching the noodle dough. And doubling it. And pulling and doubling and pulling . . .

And that was another thing to go away and talk about.

It felt as if everything was going right. But just as I was heating up the cannon *again*, there was a yell from the end of the street.

'OLLIE!'

People looked round to see what was going on – and Aunt Caz came racing towards us, her hat half-off and her sunglasses hanging from one ear. She plunged through the crowd and flung herself towards me.

'We must talk!' she hissed. 'In the van!'

I looked at the pressure gauge. 'In a minute,' I whispered back. 'I can't just –'

Aunt Caz didn't stay to listen. She pushed past me – almost bumping into the cannon – jumped into the van and slammed the door behind her.

There was something wrong. I was desperate to know what it was, but the cannon was ready to explode. Quickly I dragged the fire pit away and began to unscrew the door.

'STAND CLEAR!' I yelled.

The corn erupted into the bag. The crowd whooped with excitement – and Sam came running across.

'Go on,' he whispered. 'I'll mind your stall till you get back.'

I knew he didn't really have time. But I didn't say no – because I'd just realized something terrible. So I muttered 'Thanks!' and jumped into the van, as fast as I could.

Aunt Caz was taking off her disguise. When she heard me come in, she spun round and her mouth opened, but I didn't wait for her to speak.

'Where is he?' I hissed. 'What's happened to Gasket?'

Chapter 18
Where
Is He?

Aunt Caz shook her head frantically. 'I couldn't *stop* him, Ollie! He was very good all the time we were tracking the spy, but as soon as we got to the zoo –'

'As soon as you got to the – *what*?' I blinked.

'That's where the spy went,' Aunt Caz said. 'There's a big fence all round it and he unlocked the gate and went in. Then he locked it behind him, so I couldn't follow any more. All I could see was –'

I didn't care what she could see. 'What about *Gasket*?' I said.

Aunt Caz sat down on the bed. 'He started sniffing at the fence. Then a woman came out of one of the houses, so I went to ask her when the zoo opened, and she said it was closed for the time being and –'

'Gasket!' I said.

'When I looked round, he was squeezing under the gate. And then –' Aunt Caz bit her lip. 'Honestly, Ollie, I couldn't stop him. He . . . just vanished.'

'*Vanished?*' I didn't understand.

'One moment he was there and the next –' Aunt

Caz snapped her fingers. 'I saw him follow the spy to a big building with no windows. They must have gone inside – because that was the last time I saw him.'

'Why didn't you call his name?' I said.

'I did. A bit. But I didn't want the spy to hear me . . .'

I hadn't got time to listen to any more. I jumped out of the van and ran across to our stall. 'Quick!' I said to Sam. 'Where's the zoo?'

'The *zoo*?' Sam stared. 'It's on the other side of the island. But why on earth –'

I didn't have time to talk. 'I'll explain later. Just tell me how to get there.'

'You have to go over the hill.' He pointed. 'And then just keep going. But it's been closed for months

– ever since last year's festival, so you can't –'

'Thanks!' I dashed off, without waiting for him to finish.

If Gasket hadn't come back, he must be in trouble. He would never disappear for no reason. Either he was stuck somewhere, or else he'd been captured. Whatever it was, I had to rescue him.

If only I had the quad bike!

I ran into the big square, dodged between the stalls, and headed up the main street. There were lots of stalls there too, but I didn't even glance at them. Nothing mattered except finding Gasket, as fast as I could.

It was a long way up the hill. But once I reached the top I could see all the way to the far side of the island, with the sea beyond it, breaking on the coral reef.

The zoo was easy to spot. It was on the cliffs, right next to the sea.

But it didn't look like the zoo Sam and Daisy had described.

What had they said? *It was a lovely, happy zoo. With lots of things for the animals to do.* But I was looking down at a big expanse of concrete, full of little cages, crowded together. And behind that was a long brick building, with no windows. The only green space I could see was behind the building, and that was an overgrown wilderness, full of thick, tangled bushes.

No wonder Sam and Daisy's parents hadn't wanted to come back. The whole place looked horrible.

But the zoo was where Gasket had disappeared, so I had to get in there – somehow. I stared down at it, trying to spot a way in.

It wasn't going to be easy. There were tall railings all the way round, with only one gate – on the side facing me. I wanted to run straight down there and rattle that gate as hard as I could. Yelling Gasket's name, so he'd know I was coming to find him. But I knew that wasn't sensible. The whole place was probably full of spies who might come out and grab me. I couldn't help Gasket if I was a prisoner too.

I had to keep calm. And make a plan.

What would Beddington Potts do? I thought. He was faster than a rocket – but he didn't rush straight into danger. First of all, he thought hard – and looked carefully . . . Until he spotted a chance his enemies hadn't noticed.

So what hadn't the Duchess's spies noticed? How would Beddington Potts get into the zoo?

I stood on top of the hill, studying the fence round the zoo. On three sides, it was made of tall iron

railings, set close together. There was no chance of sneaking in that way.

But the fourth side was different.

Most of it was hidden by the long brick building, but what I could see didn't look like iron railings. More like a fence made of corrugated iron panels, running along the top of the cliffs.

I bet I could get through that, I thought. *If there's a way to reach it. Maybe there's a path up the cliffs . . . ?*

There was only one way to find out. I had to go and look. But that meant getting on to the beach without being spotted. Could I do that?

I looked at the roads leading down from the hill. The main road was wide and open, and it went straight to the zoo. If I went that way, I'd be really visible.

But if I turned left, down that little lane . . . and then right . . . and right . . . and left . . .

I followed the route with my eyes, memorizing the turns, so I didn't get lost. *Right . . . and right . . . and left . . .* Yes, that should work. I checked the route again, to make sure, and then I plunged into the maze of little streets.

The last street ran down through a gap in the cliffs, all the way to the beach. There was no one in sight, so I started walking along the beach, looking up at the cliffs to try and spot a path.

But there wasn't one. Just two huge blue pipes that ran down the cliff face, across the beach and out into the sea.

What were those for?

I had no idea. But as I got closer I saw that they were fixed to the cliff. And they looked newly painted. Whoever did that must have been able to reach all the way up. And that meant . . .

I ran along the beach to get closer and – YES! There *was* a way up! The slope was too steep for a path, but a long metal ladder was bolted to the cliff face between the two pipes.

And it went right to the top!

Gasket, here I come!

I clambered over the first pipe and started up the

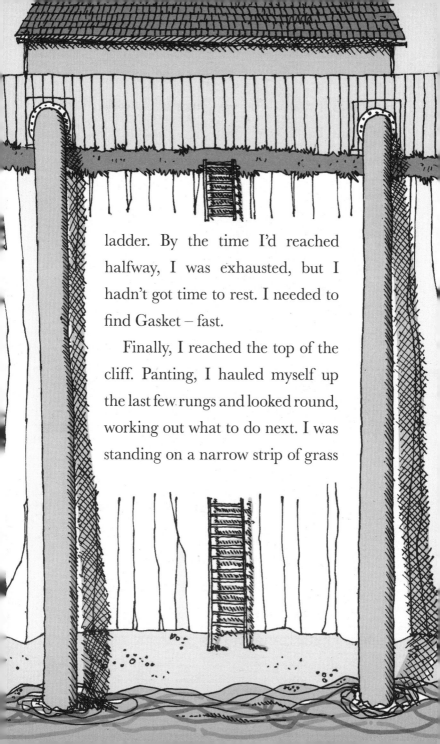

ladder. By the time I'd reached halfway, I was exhausted, but I hadn't got time to rest. I needed to find Gasket – fast.

Finally, I reached the top of the cliff. Panting, I hauled myself up the last few rungs and looked round, working out what to do next. I was standing on a narrow strip of grass at the cliff edge. The way forward was blocked by the fence I'd spotted from the top of the hill. It was too tall to see over and impossible to climb. The two

big pipes went through, but the corrugated iron fitted round them very tightly. I couldn't squeeze in that way.

I'd have to dismantle a bit of the fence.

Taking a screwdriver out of my toolbelt, I undid all the screws down one side of the nearest panel, pulled it backwards, and wriggled through.

I was in! There were bushes on the other side of the fence. I crawled through them, keeping low and following the pipes up a slope. When they reached the back of the long brick building, they disappeared through holes in the wall.

I knew where I was now. But the building was blocking the view ahead. I still couldn't see the rest of the zoo.

But I could smell it.

Chapter 19
The Zoo

The stink crept through the thickest bushes – a strong, rank smell of animals, shut up in small spaces. But there were no noises. Not a sound.

That was weird. Could all the animals be asleep?

I crept on up the slope, staying close to the side of the building, and peered round the front corner. Then I understood. The animals weren't asleep. But they were in tiny cages, with absolutely nothing to do. They looked bored and miserable. I could see lions, and penguins, anteaters, a bear and some very sad monkeys. The cages were clean and the animals looked sleek and well-fed, but their eyes were dull. And they weren't moving.

What was wrong with them?

One of the lions opened his mouth in a huge, slow yawn – and I realized.

They were *bored*.

The cages had bare concrete floors and neat shelters for the animals to sleep in, but apart from that, they were completely empty. The animals obviously got fed, but everything must have been cleared away as soon as they'd eaten. After that there was nothing for them to do except lie around yawning.

I looked along the row again – and suddenly realized that they weren't *all* holding zoo animals. The animal in the last cage was different. And he must have caught my scent, because he jumped up suddenly, looking excited. His tail started wagging and he stared towards me with eyes that were suddenly bright.

It was Gasket.

He was chained up in the cage, right out in the hot sun, with no shade or water – and they'd put a muzzle on him! For a second, I was so angry I could hardly breathe. I had to get him out of there!

But how could I unlock the cage?

Before I could think of an answer, the male lion saw Gasket staring. He jumped up too, looking in the same direction, to see what was so interesting. And then the bear noticed. And the penguins, and the anteaters and the monkeys and the lions . . .

I ducked back into a bush, with my heart thumping.

Someone was going to notice if I wasn't careful. When they saw the lions staring, they'd come to find out what was going on. Then I wouldn't have a hope of sneaking up to Gasket's cage.

What could I do?

Gasket solved the prob-
lem. He couldn't bark
– because of the muzzle
– but he started leaping
around and growling, tug-
ging at his chain to try
and get free. It was terrible
to watch. I wanted to rush
across and bend the bars
of his cage, to set him free. But that was impossible.

He was giving me the chance to make a proper plan. *That* was what I had to do.

And it was a great chance. Because what Gasket was doing must have been the most exciting thing those poor, bored animals had seen for ages. *He* couldn't make much noise – but they did!

Chapter 20
Mayhem!

The lions started roaring. That set off the monkeys in the next row of cages. They began chattering at the tops of their voices, leaping around frantically – and that started the parrots squawking and the wolves howling. The noise spread right across the zoo. Way over on the other side, I could hear the elephant trumpeting and the wild, weird laugh of a hyena.

Half a dozen people came charging out of the building. They obviously had no idea where the noise had started, or what had sparked it off, so they ran around in all directions.

This is my chance! I thought. I was just going to rush over to Gasket, when a voice came booming out over the loudspeakers.

'It's that dog from the popcorn van! He's set them off! Bring him into the aquarium building!'

The Duchess came striding across to Gasket's cage, with a little dog running behind her. She unlocked the door, unfastened Gasket's chain and started dragging him across to the building, while the terrier snapped at his feet. Gasket pulled back as hard as he could, but other people came to help. They picked

him up and carried him – still struggling – into the big brick building.

It was hard to watch without doing anything. *What are you doing with my dog?* I wanted to shout. *Let him go!* But I knew that was stupid. They'd just capture me too.

But *why*? They obviously knew where Gasket came from. So why hadn't they just brought him back to us? Why had they captured him and shut him up in that horrible cage?

Did they think he was a spy dog? Like the one who'd run into Sam and Daisy's house?

That was the only explanation I could think of. I shivered. If they were afraid of spies, there must be something secret going on in the zoo. And the only

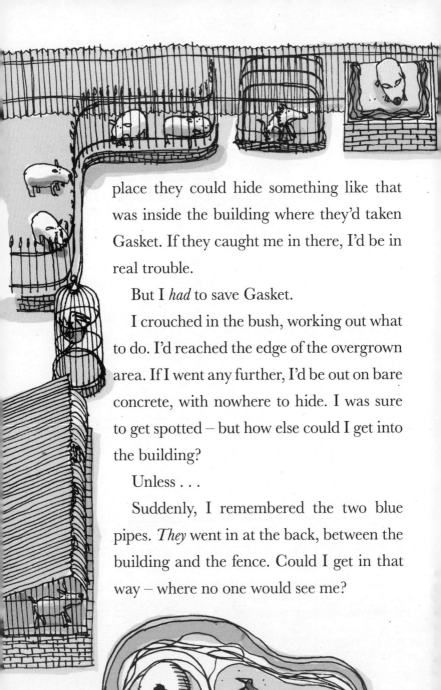

place they could hide something like that was inside the building where they'd taken Gasket. If they caught me in there, I'd be in real trouble.

But I *had* to save Gasket.

I crouched in the bush, working out what to do. I'd reached the edge of the overgrown area. If I went any further, I'd be out on bare concrete, with nowhere to hide. I was sure to get spotted – but how else could I get into the building?

Unless . . .

Suddenly, I remembered the two blue pipes. *They* went in at the back, between the building and the fence. Could I get in that way – where no one would see me?

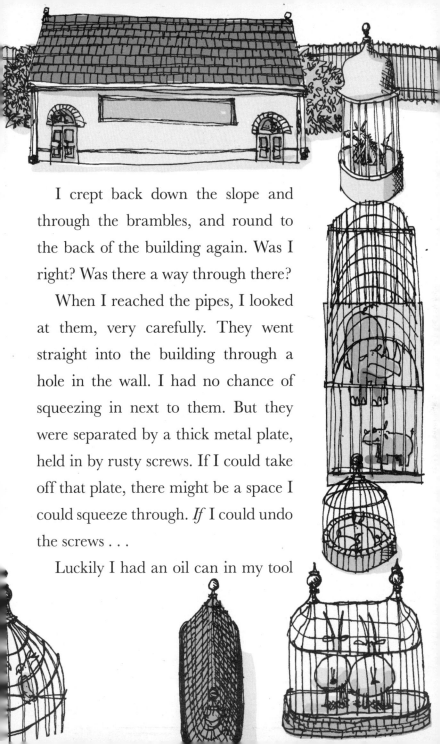

I crept back down the slope and through the brambles, and round to the back of the building again. Was I right? Was there a way through there?

When I reached the pipes, I looked at them, very carefully. They went straight into the building through a hole in the wall. I had no chance of squeezing in next to them. But they were separated by a thick metal plate, held in by rusty screws. If I could take off that plate, there might be a space I could squeeze through. *If* I could undo the screws . . .

Luckily I had an oil can in my tool

belt. I gave the screws a squirt and got to work with a screwdriver.

One screw was very stiff, but they all came out in the end. I pulled off the plate and looked through the hole.

There was a dark space ahead of me – and the pipes went different ways. The one on the right ran straight ahead, into a machine of some kind. The one on the left went up, diagonally, and disappeared through the ceiling.

For a moment I crouched silently, listening as hard

as I could. Not even breathing. Was there anyone in there?

I couldn't hear anything, so I squeezed through between the pipes (the space was *just* big enough), switched on my phone torch and looked round.

I was in a stuffy, windowless room with nothing in it except the two pipes and the machine. It looked like some kind of pump. But why would anyone be pumping water out of the sea?

For a moment, I was completely baffled. Then I got it.

The building was a saltwater aquarium!

When the water in the aquarium needed changing, clean water was pumped up, straight from the sea. And old water went out through an overflow pipe, back to the sea again.

It was a really neat arrangement. I'd have loved to stop and draw a diagram of how it all worked, but there wasn't time for that. Finding Gasket was the only thing that mattered.

I pulled the metal plate back into place between the two pipes and slipped in a couple of screws, to hold it there. Then I shone my torch around again, looking for a door.

There was only one, on the far side. I crept across and opened it, just a crack, and looked out into a small, square space. Straight ahead was a metal wall with the left-hand pipe running into it. (Maybe it was some kind of holding tank?) And on the right was a set of lift doors. Nothing else.

I didn't like the idea of using the lift. I wouldn't be able to see where I was going. When the doors opened, I might find myself facing a crowd of people. Maybe even the man in the grey coat. But there wasn't anywhere else to go, so I pressed the lift button. The doors opened immediately and I got in.

There were three floors on the control panel: *Pump Room* (that must be where I was), *Viewing Area* and *Aquarium Top*. I took a deep breath and pushed the *Viewing Area* button. The doors closed, and up I went.

It wasn't far. In a couple of seconds, the lift stopped again. The doors on the other side opened, and I stepped out into another dark lobby. It was bigger than the one I'd just left, but there was hardly room to move, because it was full of plastic boxes, stacked one on top of another. All labelled with names and addresses.

It looked as though someone was planning to post a lot of parcels.

I squeezed between the stacks, pushed open the door on the far side of the lobby, and . . .

WOW!

I was facing a glass wall, twice as tall as I was. Behind it was a huge, bright space, full of water.

I was looking into the aquarium – and it was GIGANTIC! As long as a swimming pool and much wider and deeper. There was room for a whale, or a great white shark. Or huge shoals of fish and a kelp forest.

But I couldn't see any of those.

Just . . . octopuses.

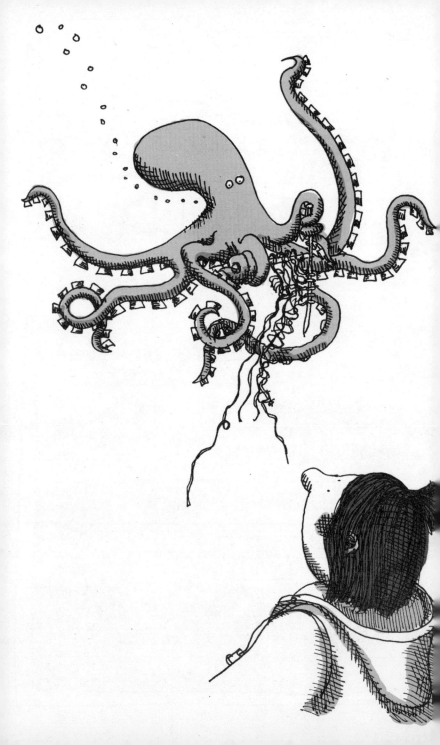

Chapter 21
The Secret of the Aquarium

The whole aquarium was full of octopuses. Maybe two hundred of them. That was weird by itself. But what they were doing was even weirder.

They weren't lying on the bottom of the aquarium. Or swimming around. Or feeding. They were waving their arms around, with the suckers clinging to long white strands of . . .

Of what? Was it some kind of water worm? Or a weird type of seaweed?

I couldn't work out what the strands were. But all the octopuses had them. And they were twisting them into loops and pulling other loops through, over and over again.

Why?

Were they getting ready to feed? Or was it some kind of game, to stop them getting bored? (*Did* octopuses get bored?) I stared into the aquarium, trying to make sense of it all.

Stop wasting time! said a panicky voice in my mind. *You need to find Gasket!*

That was right. Of course it was. Except . . .

I couldn't just charge around, hunting everywhere. I needed to understand what Gasket was doing in the zoo. *Why* had he squeezed under the gate? And when he did, why had he been captured and locked in a cage? If I didn't understand what was going on, I might make things a hundred times worse.

I stood still, trying to work it out.

The man in the grey coat *had* to be a spy. I was sure of that. And when the Duchess dragged Gasket out of the cage, there was a terrier with her. *I bet it's the terrier that ran behind Sam and Daisy's fridge*, I thought.

There was something going on in the zoo. Something *so secret* they couldn't risk anyone finding out. What was it? Could it have anything to do with the octopuses?

Pity Jin's not here, I thought. *He knows about octopuses.*

Yes! That was the answer! Jin wasn't here – but I could still ask him! I crouched down, took a couple of pictures of the octopuses, and sent them off straight away – without bothering to add a message.

The answer came zipping back in ten seconds.

Where did you find those
pictures???!!!

I didn't waste time explaining. I just asked what I wanted to know.

Any idea what they
are doing?

Knitting, of course. Great photoshopping!
I thought I'd found every . . .

Knitting! That was it!

I didn't waste time reading the rest of the message.
Jin thought it was just a joke picture – but he'd told
me what I needed to know. Those long white things
weren't worms. Or seaweed. They were *noodles*!

*AND THE OCTOPUSES WERE KNITTING
THEM INTO STRIPS.*

That was how the Duchess made the strips she
was selling! I'd been right about them being knitted underwater. But she hadn't bothered with
inventing a machine. She'd just trained octopuses to
do it instead.

She'd ruined the zoo. Built a huge aquarium. And
set up a top-secret operation, with spies and spy dogs
stealing secret recipes, and octopuses toiling away
like factory hands.

But *why*?

What was so important about selling noodles at a
food festival?

Chapter 22
The Duchess's Orders

I could hear more messages from Jin coming into my phone, but I didn't have time to read them. I turned off the sound, so it didn't give me away, and tried to work out what to do.

If only there was someone I could ask for help! But Aunt Caz had lost her phone (as usual) and everyone else I might have called was far, far away. I had to solve this problem on my own.

But before I could think of anything, I heard a

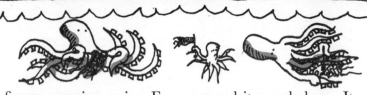

funny yapping noise. For a second it puzzled me. It didn't sound like a terrier. More like . . .

The Duchess's poodles!

It sounded as though they were just outside the door, at the far end of the Viewing Area. I had to hide – and there was only one thing I could do. I stepped back into the lift lobby and crouched behind the plastic boxes. Leaving the door ajar, so I could see what happened.

The Duchess billowed in, with the poodles trailing behind her. For a few moments she walked up and down in front of the aquarium, staring through the glass and making little disapproving clicks with her tongue. Then she shouted.

'Hethershaw!'

I heard the sound of running feet and someone else hurried in. A tall man in a grey coat. I couldn't see his face, but I guessed who it was.

'Yes, madam?' he said nervously.

'I need more noodles.' The Duchess waved her hand at the octopuses. 'Make them work faster!'

'B-but, madam,' stuttered the man, 'I don't think they can. They're already working twice as fast as they were last week.'

'If they can't work faster, then they'll have to work longer,' the Duchess said angrily. 'Cut out their feed-ing time!'

'But – they might die.' The man sounded shocked.

'Not before tomorrow night,' snapped the Duchess. 'After that, they'll be in the sea – if I win.'

'And . . . if not?' the man said nervously.

'Who cares?' The Duchess shrugged. 'Put some clams in their boxes. They can eat those while they're in the post. Stop making difficulties, Hethershaw! The important thing is I. Must. Not. Run. Out. Of.

Noodles! Make sure I don't!'

She turned round, as if she was going to march out – and the man gave an apologetic sniff.

'One more thing, madam. The dog from the popcorn van . . .'

'Yes?' The Duchess turned back, frowning.

'We've examined him,' said the man, 'and no spy devices were detected. Shall we take him to the square and let him go back to his owners?'

'Let me see him,' the Duchess said. 'I need to be sure you haven't missed anything.'

'Yes, madam.' The man started backing out of the room. 'Of course. I'll fetch him now.'

He hurried off and the Duchess stared back into the aquarium, tapping her foot impatiently.

I could hardly breathe. Would Gasket be all right? Could I grab him and run . . . somewhere? I tried to work out how and where, but it was impossible. I had no idea what was going to happen.

The man was back in a couple of minutes, dragging Gasket behind him on a chain. Gasket pulled backwards as they came through the door – but only for a couple of seconds. Once they were through, he stopped and looked around, sniffing at the air.

He was still wearing the muzzle. It was all I could do not to race through the door and wrench the chain out of the man's hands. But that would wreck everything. I clenched my fists and made myself stand still, waiting to see what happened.

The Duchess glared down at Gasket, and her little poodles danced round him, nipping at his feet. But he didn't take any notice of them. He stood very still, looking towards my hiding place.

'Have you checked inside the animal's mouth?' the Duchess said.

'We – er – we didn't think –' the man stammered.

'Well, do it now!' the Duchess said. 'Take off that stupid muzzle and make sure his mouth isn't bugged.'

Ridiculous, I thought. But the man obviously didn't dare to disagree. He let go of the chain and reached down to unstrap the muzzle . . .

But he wasn't quick enough. As soon as he dropped the chain, Gasket dashed away, racing towards my hiding place.

Chapter 23
The Tenth Year

I waved my hands at Gasket, trying to send him back. But he couldn't see them because I was hidden behind the boxes. And there was no way to shout an order without being heard. So I did the only thing that made sense.

I came out from behind the boxes, knelt down and hugged him, as hard as I could.

The Duchess looked round at the man in the grey coat. 'Who is *this person*, Hethershaw?' she said coldly.

The man looked at me. 'It's the boy from the popcorn van.'

'Spying!' The Duchess spat out the word. 'That's what you're doing, isn't it, boy?'

I stood up and looked her straight in the eye. 'Yes!' I said. 'I'm spying on you – the way you spied on the rest of us!'

'I don't know what you're talking about,' the Duchess said stiffly.

'I'm talking about that man.' I waved my hand at Hethershaw. 'He photographed Aunt Caz's list of popcorn flavourings. And you sent someone to bug Sam and Daisy's kitchen. You used your spies to steal our recipes! And lots of others too, I bet.'

'You can't prove anything,' the Duchess said. 'I just did what was necessary to win the festival prize.'

'You did all that just to win a fast-food prize?' I stared at her. 'That's *pathetic*!'

Her face turned scarlet. I thought she was going to explode. 'Stupid boy! Don't talk about things you don't understand. I *have* to win the prize this year. It's my last chance to save the island!'

I blinked. '*Save* it? From what?'

The Duchess gave a scornful sniff. 'From being *ordinary.* An unimportant, out-of-the-way place, with nothing but small farms and a pathetic little town the size of a village. If it wasn't for the food festival, we'd never see a single tourist here.'

'And you want to change that?' I didn't understand.

'By *winning the food festival*?'

Her eyes narrowed. 'My uncle started the stupid festival. He *loved* it. When he died, I found he'd left me his fortune – on one condition. I had to win the festival prize within ten years.'

Suddenly, things started making sense. 'And this is the tenth year?' I said.

'Yes it is!' the Duchess said fiercely. 'And I'm going to win – and change this island for ever!'

'You *won't* win,' I said. 'I'll tell everyone how you've cheated.'

'You won't tell anyone anything!' said the Duchess. With a mean little smile. 'Because you won't be leaving this building until I've got that prize.' She waved her hand at Hethershaw. 'Take them away and lock them in the Pump Room.'

Hethershaw looked puzzled. 'The *Pump Room*, madam?'

'It's the perfect place,' the Duchess said impatiently. 'There's no phone signal down there – and the dog can bark all he likes. No one will hear.'

Hethershaw nodded quickly. Grabbing my arm and Gasket's chain, he dragged us through the door and over to the lift. It was hard not to smile, because the Pump Room certainly *was* the perfect place – for us.

But I mustn't let him guess that, I thought. *I must make him think I'm scared. That's what Beddington Potts would do.* So I struggled and twisted, trying to tug my arm free.

But not trying *too* hard . . .

Chapter 24
What If . . . ?

I didn't stop until Hethershaw pushed us into the lift. Then I flopped sideways and looked up at him.

'What did the Duchess mean?' I asked. 'About saving the island?'

Hethershaw's eyes gleamed as he pressed the lift button. 'She'll buy up all the farms and change it into a holiday island. Full of hotels and theme parks – and a marina, for giant cruise ships. It's going to be buzzing with tourists. All year round!'

I tried to imagine it. 'But – won't that destroy the coral reef? And all the marine life?'

Hethershaw pressed the lift button. 'Who cares about *fish*?'

I wanted to argue, but it was more important to ask questions. I had to find out as much as I could. 'So what happens to the octopuses? After the festival?'

'If the Duchess wins, she won't bother selling them,' Hethershaw said. 'We'll just tip them back in the sea.'

'You mean, if she loses . . .' I remembered all those plastic boxes '. . . she'll sell them? Through the *post*?'

'Why not?' Hethershaw shrugged. 'She's got plenty of buyers waiting. Lots of people fancy an octopus in their sitting room.'

'In a little glass tank?' I shuddered. 'That's *horrible!*'

Hethershaw smirked. 'Don't worry. It's not going to happen. The Duchess is going to win that prize.'

The lift doors opened and he pulled us out and pushed us across the little lobby. I struggled a bit – so it looked as though I didn't want to be shut up.

He gave a nasty smile, opened the Pump Room door and gave me a hard shove.

'See how you like that – little spy!' he said. Then he took off Gasket's muzzle and pushed him in behind me. 'You can bark all you like now, spy dog!'

He pulled the door shut and locked it. Gasket

started barking and I banged on the door with my fists – just until I heard the lift go up again. Then I crouched down and gave Gasket a pat.

'It's all right, boy,' I whispered. 'We'll be out of here in a moment.'

He didn't understand the words, but he could hear I was OK, so he stopped barking and licked my hand. I switched on my phone torch and shone it round, reminding myself where everything was. The two pipes, the pump itself and – yes – the metal plate over on the far side.

'Come on,' I whispered. 'Now we have to be super quiet.'

I didn't want any sounds giving us away when I moved that plate.

Gasket was brilliant. He stayed totally silent, all the time I was unscrewing the plate. He followed me when I squeezed through the space and kept absolutely still while I fixed the plate back again – making sure it was secure, so no one would guess how we had escaped.

We were out of the building – but we weren't free yet.

What was I going to do about the ladder? How would I get Gasket down the cliff?

Chapter 25
Whee-ee-ee-ee!!!

I tried to work out a way to do it, as we crawled through the brambles to the corrugated iron fence. And I had lots of ideas. I could . . .

- make my sweatshirt into a sling and let it down on a rope (if only I had a rope), or
- tie Gasket on to my back (if only I had a rope) or
- hold him with one arm while I abseiled down (if only . . .)

Everything needed a rope – and that was one thing I

didn't have in my tool belt. But there must be another way to do it. We *had* to get down.

As we squeezed through the corrugated-iron fence, I was still trying to come up with an answer. But it was Gasket who found it. When he saw the pipes sloping down the cliff, his tail started wagging – and I realized.

Yes!

I hadn't even thought of the pipes. But they were the answer. I just had to work out a way to do it safely . . .

I thought about it as I did up the screws again. By the time I'd fixed the fence panel back, I knew exactly what we needed. I stood up and took off my sweatshirt.

'You have to trust me, Gasket,' I said.

He looked up at me and his tail wagged even harder.

I looped the sweatshirt under one of the pipes – with the arms in front, nearest the sea. (That was important.) Then I sat down on top of the pipe, with

a leg on each side, and patted the space in front of me.

Gasket jumped up and settled into it. I reached round him, picked up the arms of the sweatshirt, like reins, and took a deep breath.

'Here we go!'

I gave one huge push with my feet, then lifted them off the ground and –

WHEEEEEEEEEEEEEEEEEEEEEEE!

We started sliding down the pipe, slowly at first and then faster and faster –

I hauled on the arms of the sweatshirt (so we didn't slide too fast), made sure we stayed balanced (so we didn't tip sideways) and kept my arms close around Gasket (so he didn't fall off). It was like – like –

Like steering a bobsleigh! In the Olympics!

In seconds, we were at the bottom of the cliff and the pipe levelled out, with a JOLT! But we were going too fast to stop straight away. We whooshed across the beach and didn't stop until the pipe disappeared into the sea. I had to slam my feet down hard to make sure we didn't go any further.

SLOOSH! Freezing cold water splashed up all round us.

I sat still for a moment. Dripping and waiting for my heart to stop thumping. Then Gasket nudged my arm and looked round at me.

'You're right,' I said. 'We've got to get away from here.' I slithered off the pipe, snatched up the sweatshirt and squelched across the sand, with Gasket close beside me.

We had to get off the beach as fast as we could –
before someone looked down from the cliff and saw
us.

Once we reached the tangle of little streets, we
ought to be safe.

Chapter 26
The Chase

We almost made it. It was easy to run up to the high water line, because the wet sand was firm, but after that the beach was made of pebbles. They slowed us down – making a terrible noise as they rattled under our feet.

Hethershaw must have heard that. When we clambered off the beach, he was there, peering through the railings. For a second, he looked totally amazed. Then he gave a great roar and started running.

Away from the fence.

For a second, I didn't understand. Then I got it. He was heading for the main zoo gate, so he could catch us.

But we weren't going that way. We still had a chance. 'Come on, Gasket,' I panted. 'We've got to get out of sight.'

We raced down the first turning and I concentrated on not getting lost. *Left . . . right . . . left . . . left . . .* I didn't think he would find us while we were in those little streets. But what about when we reached the top of the hill? We couldn't get to the van without going down the main street and through the square.

Would we be able to hide in the crowd? Or would Hethershaw spot us?

If only I had a disguise, like Aunt Caz – and one for Gasket too. Or – even better – if I could make us *invisible*! But there was nothing I could do.

Except . . .

Suddenly, I remembered Beddington Potts. He wore lots of different disguises – but what was it he'd said in Aunt Caz's first book?

The best disguise is looking ordinary. So no one notices you.

Beddington Potts might not be real – but that sounded like good advice. If I kept running, Hethershaw would spot me straight away. I needed to look ordinary – like everyone else at the food festival.

But maybe just a bit different.

I took off my tool belt and wrapped it in my sweatshirt. Once I reached the stalls, most people would be carrying packages of food, so my 'parcel' wouldn't look too odd. No one would guess it was full of things like spanners and screwdrivers.

There was nothing I could do to disguise Gasket, but he would be hard to spot in a crowd.

'Stay close,' I whispered, as we reached the food stalls.

I had no idea where Hethershaw was. It was a struggle not to look round for him – but that would make it easier for him to notice me. I made myself slow down, looking at all the different stalls and sniffing the delicious smells. Like everyone else in the crowd.

Hethershaw would be looking for a boy on his own, so whenever we passed a family I stayed close to them for a bit. Looking as though I belonged. Trying to ignore the voice in my head.

Is Hethershaw coming up behind us? Has he spotted us?

The smell of food made me feel very hungry – and I guessed it was worse for Gasket – but I didn't dare to stop. Not even to buy pizza or burgers. Or paella or jerk chicken. Or falafel or arancini or bubble tea. We had to get back to the van.

As we turned into the main square, I spotted Hethershaw out of the corner of my eye. He was going in the same direction as we were, but I didn't think he'd seen us. I dodged round the Duchess's marquee – past a very tall man and a woman in a fancy hat – and headed for the side street where we were parked.

Slowly, slowly . . .

Once we were there, we could probably get to the van without being caught. Just a few more metres . . .

Crossing the square seemed to take hours. But at last we reached the far corner. I turned into the side street – slowly, slowly . . .

And there was a huge yell from Aunt Caz.

'Ollie! You've found Gasket!'

Chapter 27
Explosion!

The side street was full of people, all munching noodles and popcorn. Everyone turned to look as Aunt Caz pushed her way through the crowd, charging towards me.

She was almost dancing for joy. 'You're so clever, Ollie! You've found him and he looks fine thank goodness but I've been so worried even though I knew you'd sort it out because you're always so –'

The flood of words went on and on, but I couldn't

listen. Because I knew Hethershaw must be coming up behind me – and Sam and Daisy were running towards me from the other direction, shrieking at the tops of their voices.

'The cannon! Caz – you've forgotten about the cannon!'

'The pressure gauge says DANGER!'

 For a second, I didn't take in what they were saying. When I did, Hethershaw went right out of my head. Because this was MUCH WORSE. The street was full of people. If the cannon got any hotter, it might explode, and then . . .

I didn't waste time imagining what could happen. I just raced down the street, elbowed my way through the crowd and pulled the firepit out of the way.

'STAND CLEAR, EVERYONE!' I shouted.

Then I fitted the bag over the mouth of the cannon – not getting it quite right, because I was in a hurry.

Then I opened the door at the front and –

WHOOOOOOOSH! Hot popcorn sprayed out into the bag.

Well, *most* of it went in there. But because the bag wasn't on exactly right, bits of corn escaped, just missing a woman with three little children, all eating noodles.

For a moment, there was silence. Then everyone started clapping.

'Well done!' shouted the woman. 'Brilliant running!' And her children jumped up and down.

I hadn't got my breath back enough to answer, but I managed to smile – until I saw Hethershaw.

The crowd had blocked his path when they backed
away from the cannon. But he'd seen me. And he was
heading straight towards me, crunching over stray
bits of popcorn.

Where could I go? I could run into the van – but
that was the first place he'd look. And if I went anywhere else, he would follow. There was no way I
could escape. Hethershaw was going to catch me and
make sure I didn't tell anyone about the octopuses.
There was no time –

And then the seagulls swooped.

Chapter 28
Seagulls

Half a dozen of them had spotted the scattered popcorn and they came screeching down to peck it up, snapping and squabbling as they fought over it.

The woman at the front backed away, pulling her children with her. The children dropped their noodles. The man next to them skidded on the noodles, knocking two people over and crashing into four or five others.

Suddenly, everyone was backing away, trying to

avoid the chaos – and more people were slipping and sliding. One of them bumped into Hethershaw and sent him staggering backwards. He stumbled against the tall man and the woman in the fancy hat, who were just coming up behind him.

The woman shouted, and Hethershaw lost his footing – and fell into the middle of the crowd.

That was my chance to escape!

While everyone was looking the other way, picking people up, I jumped into Sam and Daisy's caravan, with Gasket close behind me. I locked the door, as quickly as I could, hoping Sam and Daisy wouldn't mind. There was nowhere else I could go.

Then I flopped down on to the bench and gave a huge sigh of relief. While I was catching my breath – and trying to think what to do next – I heard my phone ping and I pulled it out of my pocket, expecting a message.

But there wasn't just one message. There were *sixteen* of them.

All from Jin.

Chapter 29

'You Have
to do
Something!'

I stared at the screen for a second. Then I went to the top and started scrolling down. Every single message was about the picture I'd sent him.

Thought I'd seen every bluetop octopus photo on the internet.

I've done another web search. Can't track that image down anywhere.

Where did you find it???

It HAS to be computer-generated. Right?

No one's ever seen that many bluetops at once.
There must be two hundred!

TELL ME OLLIE! IT'S DRIVING ME MAD!!!

The messages went on and on, but I couldn't read any more. My mind was exploding.

The octopuses I'd seen weren't really blue – just a kind of dingy bluish grey. But Jin sounded absolutely sure they were bluetops – the reason he was raising money. The scientists at Free the Sea were trying to discover why all the bluetops had suddenly disappeared from the ocean – *and I knew the answer.*

THEY WERE ALL IN THE DUCHESS'S AQUARIUM.

The Duchess had captured two hundred of the world's rarest, most intelligent octopuses – and trained them to knit noodles. And she didn't care if they died.

For a moment, it seemed too weird to be true. Then I remembered all the other things she'd done. The spies she'd sent out. The recipes she'd stolen. The zoo she'd ruined.

She was *desperate* to win the festival prize – and now I knew why. I typed a reply to Jin, as fast as I could.

> Those bluetops are REAL.
> I took the picture today.

I was expecting another message in return, but that was too slow for Jin. Half a second later, my phone started ringing and Jin began talking as soon as I answered.

'This is a wind-up. Right, Ollie? There are at least TWO HUNDRED bluetops in that picture. You're not seriously saying –'

I didn't wait for him to finish. 'It's not a joke! I *saw* those octopuses, Jin. And I know it sounds weird, but they really *are* knitting noodles. What should I do?'

'Call the police!' Jin said. As if that was obvious. 'Bluetops are a protected species.'

'But . . .' I hesitated. Calling the police felt like a bad idea. 'That aquarium belongs to the Duchess. And she runs this island. The police might not even listen to me. And if they do, and they tell her . . .' I shuddered. 'What about those Free the Sea people? The ones you're raising money for. Can't you tell them?'

'Of *course* I'll tell them,' Jin said. 'And they'll send some of their eco-warriors. But it'll take them a couple of days to reach you.'

'Then they'll be too late!' I said. 'The Duchess is going to stop feeding the octopuses, so they knit more noodles. She doesn't care if they don't live past Sunday night.'

'WHAT?' For a second, Jin was speechless with fury. 'Ollie, those are probably the only bluetops left in the *whole* world. And Free the Sea can't possibly get there before Sunday night. You'll have to rescue them yourself!'

'But how?'

'Just get them into the sea. Somehow. They'll be fine once they're there. The sea round that island is a great bit of bluetop habitat. There's even a coral reef.' Jin sighed impatiently. 'Come on, Ollie. It can't be *that* hard to move a few octopuses.'

Harder than getting Gasket out, I thought. *I can't slide two hundred octopuses down on my sweatshirt.*

'Once they're in the sea they'll be safe.' Jin said.

No they won't! Not if the Duchess wins the festival prize. She'll build that marina – and the giant cruise ships will ruin everything.

I nearly said that out loud. But I hadn't got time to explain it all to Jin. I needed to *think*.

'OK,' I said. 'I'll make a plan and call you back.'

I hung up and looked down at Gasket. And he looked up at me, with his ears pricked and his eyes sharp and bright – almost as if he understood how complicated it was.

Jin was right – I *had* to get the bluetops back in the sea.

BUT not if the Duchess won the festival prize – because she'd build the marina and ruin the sea.

SO I needed to make sure – somehow – that she *didn't* win.

EXCEPT – if she didn't win, she'd send the bluetops off in those horrible little boxes. And they'd *never* get back to the sea.

'It's impossible, Gasket!' I said. 'I can't save them, whatever I do.'

And then someone rattled the door handle . . .

Chapter 30
Rule Six

'Ollie?' called Sam's voice. 'Are you in there?'

I went to the window and lifted the curtain, just a few centimetres. There was no sign of Hethershaw, so I unbolted the door and Sam slipped in.

'Sorry,' I said, 'but I was being followed – it was the spy who stole our recipes – and I was trying to think – and I have to . . .' I didn't know where to start.

'Sit down,' Sam said. 'Take a deep breath. OK? Now, begin at the beginning.'

I sat down on the bench. 'OK,' I said. 'You know Aunt Caz went off to follow the spy? I sent Gasket with her – and he got trapped in the zoo. So I went to find him and I had to find a way in . . .'

As I explained, Sam's eyes opened wider and wider. When I got to the bit about the octopuses, his mouth opened too, as if he couldn't believe it.

'It's *true*,' I said. I pulled out my phone and found the photo I'd sent to Jin. 'Look!'

Sam stared at the photo for a moment, without saying anything. Then he looked up at me. 'If that's really how the Duchess makes her noodles, she's broken Rule Six.'

I blinked. 'Rule Six?'

'It's meant to stop big companies winning the festival prize.' Sam chanted the words. *'Only snacks made by the stallholders themselves shall be eligible for the festival prize.'*

'You mean – the Duchess cheated?' I said.

Sam nodded.

I felt like cheering. 'So all we have to do is tell the judges . . .'

But Sam wasn't smiling. 'We've just missed them. They were here half an hour ago, but now they've gone off to their hotel – to decide the marks.'

'So we go to the hotel, now, and tell them,' I said, starting to get up.

Sam pushed me gently back down. 'No chance,' he said. 'Security is super tight at the hotel. They can't risk any sabotage, there's no way you'll get to see them. They'll stay shut up in there until tomorrow, when they come out to announce the winner.'

'So?' I said. 'We'll tell them then.'

Sam frowned. 'No chance there either. They'll

be up on the stage, with music playing and all the tourists yelling. We won't be able to get near – and no one will hear if we shout.'

I didn't understand. 'But – if it's that noisy, how *can* they announce the winner?'

'The results get projected up on the marquee. And everyone goes *wild*.' Sam shook his head. 'Nobody's going to listen to us, Ollie. We've missed our chance.'

No. There *had* to be a way. I closed my eyes and tried to think. For a moment, my mind was completely blank.

Then I remembered what Sam had said. *The results get projected up on the marquee.*

I opened my eyes again. 'Who's in charge of the projector?'

Sam looked puzzled. 'Mum's cousin Ferdy. But why –'

'Could you speak to *him*? Before tomorrow?'

'Yes, of course. But I don't see . . .'

I chewed my lip, working things out. We could stop the Duchess winning, if Cousin Ferdy helped us.

But that wouldn't save the octopuses. Unless . . .

Suddenly I had a wild, crazy idea.

'Sam, how does the aquarium work?' I said. 'I mean – when they pump new water up from the sea, why doesn't everything in the aquarium disappear down the overflow pipe, with the old water?'

'There's a grille,' Sam said. 'Across the opening of the overflow pipe.'

'And that grille – does it come off?' I was pretty sure I knew the answer. But I had to be certain.

'Of course. When it needs cleaning . . .' Sam's eyes opened wide. 'Do you mean . . . ?'

I nodded. 'I know how we can save the octopuses – and the island too.'

Chapter 31
The False Trail

We had to wait until the stalls closed to talk to Daisy and Aunt Caz. At eleven o'clock that night, the four of us sat round the table in our van and I explained my plan.

By the time I'd finished, Aunt Caz was very, *very* excited. 'You're going on a secret mission!' she said. '*Just* like Beddington Potts!'

'Except . . .' Daisy said. And stopped.

I looked at her. 'Except what?'

Daisy frowned. 'You and Sam can't set the octopuses free until you're sure the Duchess hasn't won. But she might decide to post them off *right away*. And if she heads straight for the aquarium, in her car –'

Sam nodded, pulling a face. 'She'll get there before we've finished.'

He was right. We couldn't risk that. But there had to be a way . . .

What would Beddington Potts do? I thought.

'Beddington Potts would distract her!' Aunt Caz said. As if she'd read my mind. 'Suppose she thinks we're attacking the *front* of the zoo –'

'– with the popcorn cannon!' Daisy started laughing.

She was joking, but Aunt Caz's eyes lit up. 'That's it!' she said. 'I'll load the cannon into the van and park in the square. And the moment they announce the winner I'll shout, "TO THE ZOO!" and drive off. Very fast!'

'We'll stand near the spies!' Daisy said. 'To make sure they notice us leaving!'

'And we'll get everything ready tonight!' Aunt Caz was grinning now. 'So when we get to the zoo . . .'

'. . . the keepers will come running!' Daisy punched the air.

She and Aunt Caz were so excited they couldn't stop talking. When Sam went back to the caravan, they were still planning what to do at the zoo gate. To make sure there was no one left in the aquarium.

I climbed into my bunk, hoping they got it right. Because our plan *had* to work.

It was the octopuses' only chance.

Chapter 32
The Prize-Giving

The prize-giving was due to start at four o'clock the next afternoon.

At three o'clock, Sam and I slipped away, leaving Daisy and Aunt Caz to get the van ready. By ten to four, we were down on the beach, hiding between the two pipes.

Waiting for Daisy to call us.

The phone signal was just strong enough down there. Daisy called from the main square at four o'clock. Exactly. She didn't waste time talking. She just held up her phone – like everyone else in the crowd – to let us see what was happening.

The stage in front of the Duchess's marquee was draped in purple velvet. There were two golden lecterns set in the middle of the stage and behind them were huge letters, projected on to the side of the marquee.

People certainly *did* cheer. The noise was so loud I turned down the sound on my phone. Everyone in the crowd was yelling and the trumpets blared as two figures climbed on to the stage.

The very tall man. And the woman in the fancy hat.

If only I'd known *they* were the judges! I could have told them about the octopuses when I was running away from Hethershaw.

But it was too late to think about that. We had to concentrate on our plan. I held my phone steady, so Sam could see the picture.

The words on the marquee changed. Now they said:

TOP THREE STALLS – FINAL SCORES:
TASTE
CAZ'S PERFECT POPCORN – 5
THE DUCHESS'S KNITTED NOODLES – 5
BELINDA'S BLISSFUL ICE CREAM – 5

More cheering. But Sam and I didn't make a sound. We held our breath as the next set of marks went up:

TEXTURE
THE DUCHESS'S KNITTED NOODLES – 5
NED AND NORA'S NOODLES – 5
HENRY'S TOASTED BAGELS – 5

The cheering wasn't so loud this time. But the Duchess didn't care. We could see her sitting just below the stage, with two little poodles on her lap. Smirking as the next set of marks went up.

ORIGINALITY
THE DUCHESS'S KNITTED NOODLES – 5
CAZ'S PERFECT POPCORN – 5
SALLY'S STUFFED CUCUMBERS – 5

The results seemed to go on and on. But finally the words we were waiting for appeared on the side of the marquee:

AND THE WINNER IS . . .

The crowd was totally silent now, as if people were holding their breath. No one moved – except the Duchess. She rose to her feet, tipping the dogs off her lap, and raised her arms in triumph as she waited for her name to appear.

But it didn't.

Instead, a photograph was projected on the side of the marquee. The cheering stopped as people stared up at the rows of octopuses – knitting noodles.

The judges looked puzzled for a moment. Then they turned round to look at the marquee. They started whispering together and then they bent down and spoke to the Duchess.

We couldn't hear what she said, but we saw her stamping and shaking her fist. The tall man

straightened up and went to talk to someone at the side of the stage.

'That's Ferdy,' Sam whispered.

I held my breath. Was it going to work?

The tall judge walked back to the lectern and spoke into the microphone. I turned the sound on my phone right up, to make sure we could hear.

'It appears that Rule Six has been broken,' the judge said. 'The stallholder with the highest score denies her noodles were knitted by octopuses – but

she refuses to explain to us how they *were* knitted. So there is only one thing for us to do.' He waved his hand at Ferdy, and huge letters flashed on to the photograph.

DISQUALIFIED!

'That's it!' I said. 'Come on, Sam!'

We didn't wait to see anything else. I pushed my phone into my pocket – there was no signal where we were going! – and started climbing the metal ladder as fast as I could. With Sam right behind me.

Chapter 33
The Attack on the Gates

We were almost at the top by the time we heard the van coming down the hill, racing at top speed. The brakes squealed as it pulled up in front of the zoo gates and we heard Aunt Caz and Daisy jump out.

'Hurry,' I said to Sam, over my shoulder. 'They'll be setting the cannon up now. We need to be ready by the time it's hot.'

I threw myself towards the corrugated iron fence, taking out the screws as fast as I could and pulling the panel open for Sam to squeeze through. I didn't waste time putting the screws back this time. It was our last chance to settle things.

We crawled up the slope, making sure we didn't make any noise. When we reached the building, I unscrewed the metal plate that would let us in, but we didn't squeeze in. We had to wait for the right moment.

Creeping to the side of the building, we peered round the corner at the front gates.

Aunt Caz and Daisy had set up the popcorn cannon

just outside the gates and the firepit was beginning to blaze. I could see Gasket beside it, standing very still, with his nose lifted. He was staring towards me – but he didn't move. *Stay with Aunt Caz*, I'd said. So that's what he was doing.

I'd been expecting all that. What I hadn't expected was the people.

Aunt Caz and Daisy must have left the prize-giving VERY dramatically, because lots of people had obviously followed, to see what was going to happen. There was a crowd behind them and a line of cars and vans crawling down from the top of the hill – with the Duchess's car trapped in the middle.

That was perfect! But Sam and I couldn't move yet. We had to be sure there were no zoo keepers inside the aquarium. So we waited, while the cannon got hotter.

And hotter. And hotter . . .

Until Daisy shouted, 'Here we go!'

She bent down, unscrewed the door and opened it wide – *without fitting the bag on.*

The popcorn exploded out of the cannon, shooting straight through the zoo gates in a long, steaming streak. There was a huge cheer, as people watched it spraying across the concrete inside the zoo and I held my breath. Had I guessed right

about what would happen now?

YES!

Seagulls came swooping down on to the popcorn, flapping and screeching. But this time there weren't just half a dozen of them. There were hundreds – all pecking at the ground and squabbling with each other.

Now – Gasket! I thought.

Daisy was ready. She bent down and whispered to Gasket and he crawled under the gate and charged at the seagulls.

They whirled up and away from him – and then back down to the popcorn. Over and over again. The air was full of wings and feathers and wild, angry squawks and the noise didn't stop. And Gasket kept chasing round, barking at the top of his voice.

That started the lions roaring in their cages. And the elephant trumpeted. And the wolves howled. And the whole zoo went wild!

The zookeepers heard THAT. They came running from all over the zoo – and out of the aquarium. Just the way we'd planned. They started racing around, trying to catch Gasket and scare off the seagulls.

'Now!' I whispered to Sam.

We ran round to the back of the building and squeezed through the narrow space between the pipes. There was no need to say anything. We both knew exactly what we needed to do.

Sam headed straight for the lift and zoomed up to take the grille off the overflow pipe. And I crouched down beside the pump. Concentrating hard to make sure I did everything right.

Because we only had one chance.

I felt for the valves on each side of the pump, open-ing them as wide as they would go. Then I switched the pump on, at full speed. For a split second, nothing

happened. Then the pump started chugging away.

Pumping water up from the sea.

I put my hand on the pipe for a moment, just to feel it vibrating. Then I headed out into the lift and went up the Viewing Area.

And the lobby with its stack of nasty plastic boxes.

I shivered as I went past them, imagining the octopuses packed into those tiny little spaces. *We have to save them!* I thought. *We HAVE to.*

By the time I reached the Viewing Area, Sam was already back from the Aquarium Top – looking damp and bedraggled.

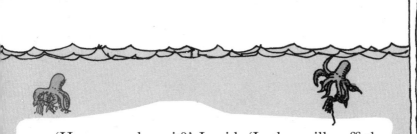

'Have you done it?' I said. 'Is the grille off the pipe?'

He nodded, without looking round. He was staring at the octopuses.

'It's true, isn't it?' he whispered. 'They really *are* knitting the Duchess's noodles.'

'Not for much longer,' I whispered back.

I took a step back, looking up at the top of the tank. I could see the opening of the overflow pipe, still half a metre above the water. The water level was rising – but how long would it take to reach that opening?

Had we got enough time?

Sam and I stared up, watching the water creep higher, centimetre by centimetre. Willing it to rise faster . . .

It was almost there – but not quite – when we heard another screech of brakes. Then someone roared 'Out of my way!'

The seagulls squawked, Gasket barked – and the door of the aquarium flew open.

'What are you doing in here?' bellowed a furious voice.

Chapter 34
Operation Bluetop

It was the Duchess.

I looked at Sam, just for an instant. He got it straight away.

We had to stop the Duchess noticing the water level. Sam flung himself forward, shaking his fist at her. 'You've ruined this zoo!' he yelled. 'All those, animals, shut up in tiny cages – it's *cruel*!'

'And the elephant!' I shouted. 'Can't you *see* how miserable she is!'

'And the wolves!' shrieked Sam. 'And the penguins!'

It *almost* worked. The Duchess blinked and took a step back. For a couple of seconds, she looked from me to Sam and back again. I could see her getting angrier and angrier. *Good!* I thought.

But suddenly she frowned – as if she was puzzled – and looked down at the floor.

Oh no! Had she noticed the sound of the pump?

She had. And one quick look at the aquarium told her what was happening.

'Stupid little meddlers!' she snarled, pushing us out of the way as she ran towards the lift.

My heart sank. The water level was *almost* at the overflow pipe now. But she still had time to get to the Aquarium Top. Time to put the grille back over the opening.

If she did that, the octopuses would never escape.

Sam and I grabbed at her arms, but she was stronger and heavier than we were and she shook us off. She was almost at the lift door.

But as she reached up to press the button, a shape came charging in, racing towards her. It was Gasket! With the Duchess's poodles panting along behind him.

Gasket jumped up at the Duchess, knocking her backwards, away from the lift. The little dogs raced round excitedly, knocking over the plastic boxes. The Duchess lost her balance, staggered across the floor and  crashed into the front of the tank.

Just as the water level reached the overflow pipe.

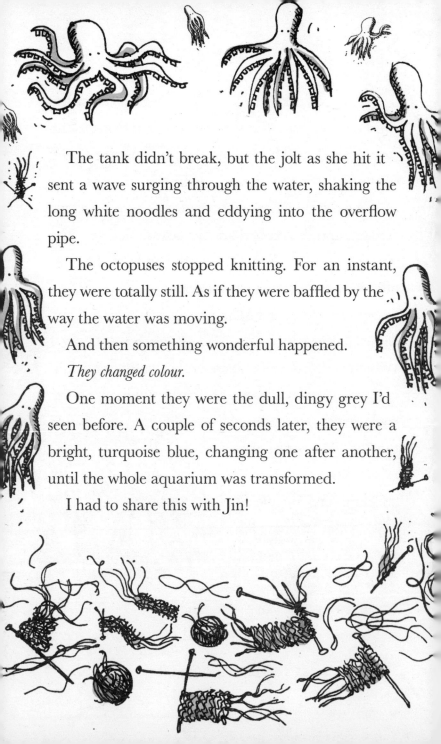

The tank didn't break, but the jolt as she hit it sent a wave surging through the water, shaking the long white noodles and eddying into the overflow pipe.

The octopuses stopped knitting. For an instant, they were totally still. As if they were baffled by the way the water was moving.

And then something wonderful happened.

They changed colour.

One moment they were the dull, dingy grey I'd seen before. A couple of seconds later, they were a bright, turquoise blue, changing one after another, until the whole aquarium was transformed.

I had to share this with Jin!

I took out my phone, as fast as I could, and started filming as the octopuses let go of their knitting. The noodles drifted down to the bottom of the tank in a tangled, doughy mess – and the octopuses went *up*!

One after another, they jetted across the aquarium in a long turquoise streak, up through the water and into the mouth of the overflow pipe.

They'd found it!

By the time the Duchess got her balance back, it was too late to stop them. They were all disappearing into the pipe, on their way to freedom. Gasket licked my hand, wagging his tail as hard as he could, and I bent down and hugged him.

'Well done, boy! *Well done!*'

Chapter 35
It's Our
Island Now!

As the last octopus disappeared into the pipe, Sam punched the air.

'We did it, Ollie! They're free!'

The Duchess almost spat with rage. 'Ridiculous! Those octopuses belong to *me*! What use are they now?'

'They belong to themselves,' I said. 'They don't have to be useful.'

'Sentimental nonsense!' The Duchess glared at us

both. 'You've stolen my property – and I'm going to call the police!'

Sam looked worried, but I wasn't scared. 'Yes, call the police!' I said. 'Then I can tell them about the things *you* stole. You're a thief as well as a cheat. And you tried to win the festival prize under false pretences. I can't wait to tell the police all about it!'

The Duchess blinked and took a step back. For a moment, she was speechless. Then she tossed her head scornfully. 'Don't bother! I'm through with this piffling little island. Let the islanders keep their stupid farms and their one-horse town, if that's the way they like it!'

One of the poodles came yapping round her feet and she kicked out at it and stamped off through the door.

'Don't forget your dogs!' Sam called after her.

The Duchess looked back at the poodles. 'Keep up!' she snarled. 'We're leaving on the next ferry!' She opened the door and stormed out.

That was when we heard the noises from outside.

The seagulls were still squabbling, but we could hardly hear them now. Their squawks were drowned out by the sound of voices cheering and singing. Sam and I looked at each other. Gasket started barking and we all headed for the door.

The road outside the zoo was full of people. Hundreds of them. They were laughing and talking and chanting happily.

'It's our island now!'

'Safe at last!'

'We'll make it perfect!'

The Duchess stamped towards the gate, glowering at them all. Her car was still boxed in, blocked by

dozens of cars behind it, but she didn't stop. Flinging the gates open, she pushed her way through the crowd and disappeared up the hill, her long purple skirts trailing in the dust.

As soon as she had gone, people flooded into the zoo, crunching over the popcorn and shaking their heads when they saw the animals shut up in tiny cages.

'We need your mum and dad!' one of them shouted to Sam. 'They *have* to come back and make the zoo right again!'

'The island council will pay them!' someone else yelled to Daisy. 'Ask them now!'

Daisy pulled out her phone and Sam ran towards her, to join in the conversation. I looked down at Gasket. 'Seems as though everything's working out,' I said. 'Let's go and find Aunt Caz.'

That was easy. She was shouting the loudest of all, trying to answer everyone's questions at once.

'. . . it was lucky we had the cannon . . . yes, Ollie had a secret way in . . . he and Sam rescued the octopuses . . . yes, they're REALLY rare . . .'

She didn't even notice me until I pulled at her sleeve. Then she turned round and beamed at me and Gasket.

'Ollie! We did it!'

I nodded, and the people round Aunt Caz started clapping and shouting.

'You deserve a prize!'

'We'll have a party this evening!'

'Stay for a week!'

It all sounded like fun. But Aunt Caz sighed. 'We have to leave NOW,' she said. 'On the next ferry. Ollie needs to be back for school tomorrow.'

'Aw, Aunt Caz,' I said. 'Can't we just –'

She shook her head firmly. 'I *promised*, Ollie. We have to go.'

'Two minutes!' I said.

Before she could answer, I ran across to say goodbye to Sam and Daisy. They both had huge smiles on their faces.

'Mum and Dad are VERY happy,' Daisy said. 'And they can't wait to meet you, Ollie.'

I shook my head. 'Sorry, I've got to go. Maybe another time?'

'Come back in the holidays!' said Sam. 'Then you can see the zoo the way it used to be, and we can go snorkelling on the reef, and introduce you to Ada, the elephant, and –'

'OLLIE!' Aunt Caz shrieked. 'Come and load up the cannon – or we'll miss the ferry!'

Sam and Daisy came with me, still talking about all the things we could do next time I visited. They hadn't finished when I slammed the boot shut and jumped into the van.

'. . . and Gasket can help us train the poodles!' Daisy yelled.

'Yes! YES!' I shouted. Gasket and I leaned out of the window and waved, all the way up the hill.

Chapter 36
Home Again

The ferry doors were just closing as Aunt Caz drove on to the jetty.

'Shout, Ollie!' she said. 'Tell them we're coming!'

I leaned out of the window and waved as hard as I could. 'Please wait! We need to catch this ferry!'

Gasket leaned out too, barking at the top of his voice. Between us, we managed to attract their attention. The doors opencd again, the van swept along the jetty and we just made it on to the boat.

Aunt Caz parked and turned off the engine.

'Time for a snack!' she said.

We went up into the passenger lounge. There were lots of stallholders up there, on their way back from the festival. Everyone was very friendly and they were all sharing out their leftover food. Aunt Caz and I ate Flora's Fritters and Donald's Doughnuts, Sindy's Soup and Ivan's Ice Cream – and all kinds of other delicious things.

The Duchess was sitting on the far side of the lounge, ignoring everyone. She was wearing huge dark glasses and her poodles were crouched by her feet, shivering unhappily.

'What d'you think she'll do now?' I whispered to Aunt Caz.

'She's got questions to answer,' Aunt Caz whispered back. 'The way she treated those animals in the zoo was disgusting. So I phoned the police before we left . . .'

She didn't say any more. But when the ferry reached the mainland, the Duchess stormed off the boat, dragging the poodles behind her – and she didn't get far. There was a police car parked on the quay and two police officers came walking down the jetty to meet her.

We had to go down to the car deck then, so I didn't see exactly what happened next. But when we drove off the ferry, the police car was gone – and so was the Duchess.

'Good riddance!' said Aunt Caz, as we headed for the motorway. 'Now let's get you back in time for school. I think we can do it – if I drive all night.'

I settled down in my seat, with Gasket's head on my lap – and my eyes started closing. That's the last thing I remember until I was woken up by the sound of the horn, honking furiously. I sat up and looked out of the window.

It was morning. And the van was just pulling up outside our house.

'There you are!' Aunt Caz said triumphantly.

'You've even got time for breakfast before you have to go to school.'

Everyone came racing out of the house.

'Did you have a good time?'

'Have you brought us lots of snacks?'

'Did people like the cannon?'

Before I had a chance to answer, I heard brakes squealing and a bell ringing and tyres screeching – and Jin came hurtling round the corner on his bike.

'You did it!' he yelled when he saw me. 'You saved the bluetops! I want to hear ALL about it!'

The cousins all stared at him.

'What?' said Arabella.

'WHAT?' said Ellie and Zak and Lulu.

I was still wondering how to answer when Mum ran out and grabbed my arm. 'Breakfast. Now,' she

said. 'You're not going to school till you've had your porridge.'

She swept us all into the kitchen and dished out bowls of porridge to everyone. And while we were eating that, Jin got a video from Free the Sea.

'Look!' he said, holding out his phone. 'Look, Ollie! The eco-warriors finally got to the island. And when they dived, they saw – just LOOK!'

He held out his phone – and there were the blue-tops. Dozens and dozens of them, swimming around the coral reef. And they were still the same beautiful, bright turquoise colour. Every single one of them.

'We have to go there!' Jin said. 'As soon as it's the holidays. I want to go snorkelling. So I can see them for myself.'

'Yes!' shouted all the cousins. 'Can we come too? We want to go snorkelling!'

Jin looked at me and I grinned and nodded. Thinking, *Could I make a snorkelling mask for Gasket? So he could come too . . . ?*

I didn't have a chance to work out how, because Jin went on asking questions. He was so excited that he didn't stop when Mum shouted at us.

'Time for school! Hurry up, you two.'

Jin threw his bike into the van and went on talking as Aunt Caz drove us there. 'Sam said *what*? . . . But how did you stop the Duchess winning the festival prize? . . . And the bluetops really changed colour?'

I was so busy answering his questions that I didn't think about anything else. Not until we'd reached school and I'd patted Gasket and jumped out of the van. Then I realized I had a question of my own.

'Hey! Aunt Caz!' I yelled, as Gasket jumped back in the van.

She stuck her head out of the window. 'What?'

'Who *did* win the festival prize?' I shouted.

Aunt Caz grinned. 'We did, of course!'

And she tooted the horn and screeched away up the road.

About the Author

GILLIAN CROSS was born in London. Writing stories for children is her main job, but she has done lots of other interesting jobs, including teaching, assisting a baker and advising the government about libraries and how important they are. Gillian has written many award-winning books, and her bestselling *Demon Headmaster* series has been dramatized for television. She has travelled round the world talking to readers about her books, and her adventures have taken her to exciting places like Belgium, Sweden, Brazil and Australia. In her spare time, Gillian likes to play the piano, swim, garden, orienteer (which involves finding your way round forests with a map) and, of course, read lots of books.

About the Illustrator

ALAN SNOW was born in Kent. Before becoming an award-winning author and illustrator, he had many different jobs, including yogurt flavour mixer, tree surgeon (someone who looks after trees), and car/robot/wedding dress designer (but not all at the same time). He has written and illustrated lots of books for children, including a magical adventure called *Here Be Monsters!* This was made into a very successful cartoon film called *The Boxtrolls*, which was nominated for lots of awards, including an Oscar for Best Animated Feature film. Alan has recently spent time designing an ice-cream parlour, drawing inspiration from Willy Wonka's chocolate factory.